WIN
LOSE
RISE
FALL

TALLIA FURY

UK BookPublishing.com

Editing, design, typesetting and publishing by UK Book Publishing

www.ukbookpublishing.com

ISBN: 978-1-916572-76-8

WIN
LOSE
RISE
FALL

CHAPTER ONE

The house stood proud in the once sleepy Scottish village where nothing ever happened; but changes had led the family away from their expected paths, known for respectability, then notoriety and fame.

The house held them captive and upset the course of their lives if they tried to leave. Marguerite, mother and grandmother, couldn't explain, but thought the garden somehow seemed to have magical powers. The mountains, often covered in snow, were an envied view that could be seen more fully from the upstairs balcony, which extended from the main bedroom. Chevelly House was large and predominantly built from terracotta bricks with different colours chequered through and the drive was full of all the family's cars.

The fences had been replaced with higher fences before anyone could look in; they now wanted to avoid peering eyes. They were white and had been painted this year, which was a good sign; if they were grey, it meant that all was not well. It was a cold winter, but maybe not the coldest she had known.

Her roles were now eight as another granddaughter, the second child of her eldest daughter, had joined them. One to four were to her two daughters and two sons; five was her husband's wife though now divorced, a role that had to be considered; six, seven, and eight as grandmother to her grandchildren.

Her first daughter's life was about her children and pursuing a partner worthy to take her from the house. Several had tried but had always returned.

Her second daughter had chosen to put her energies into her career as a fashion designer, which had brought her fame and fortune but was not good for her relationships.

Her sons were now men; her first had been a trial over the years and had caused unprecedented problems, taking that role from her eldest daughter to a new level. Her second son, always in his brother's shadow, had surprised everyone by becoming a boxer and had done well.

Her grandson and her first granddaughter had different personalities, but close friends and cousins were always stronger in diversity than similarities.

Lastly, her second granddaughter joined the house, a mystery, and they were still waiting to find out how she would impact the house. They were, it seemed, in a settled stage, and Christmas was again approaching.

Marguerite looked at herself in the mirror which was still by the door. Everyone checked themselves there before answering the door or leaving the house. She was a little more rounded now, having been thin before and even gaunt, but now was as she should be.

She had been lucky enough years back to buy a haberdashery shop where she had been an employee, and it had been a stepping stone for her and more so for her second daughter whose business had started there; then, eventually, a workshop had been built on the back of the shop with the help of her eldest daughter's boyfriend who had decided to try and impress her daughter by completing a task he had started, it became inadequate and was now an extension of the shop and the bay window now displayed cloths and fabrics that she changed each season, artistically picking up the feel and colour. The two mannequins, a boy and a girl designs, weren't needed and the shop gave her a good income; the assistant she employed had stayed and she could trust her and take the time she needed where before she had little time for anything, and perhaps it had cost her her relationship with the man who had cost her her marriage – she had had many years with him, but eventually they had parted. She was single at the moment but that would change – she wasn't a woman not to have a man in her life, she had a few potentially serious relationships but they hadn't been right for various reasons. She had learnt a lot, was wiser and ready for what could take her into retirement with a partner, but it was not an easy place to fill.

CHAPTER TWO

PAST RELATIONSHIPS

Her first daughter Maisie was in her early thirties, very tall with blonde hair, a mother with a boy now fourteen and a daughter aged four. Her son's father had left after they had been together for eight years. She had never been sure whether he had returned to an old girlfriend. The one time they – her sister, her brothers, her son, and her sister's daughter – spent Christmas with her father and girlfriend, he had not been invited. It could have been that which had furthered the decline. He accused her of having no time for him and not being prepared to leave the house to move with him and he didn't want to stay at the house without her and made the long journey to visit his family who lived in England. They had met when he moved to Scotland with his work, but he had caused trouble to the family, and they broke up later. He had managed to regain her interest by always being at the college gates. When she was leaving, she was often with a foreign boy. He had followed them once to the park but then decided that he would wait until she was on her own and after a few more days of waiting at the gates, she had been. She agreed to let him say what he wanted and said how sorry he was. Maisie was annoyed that her boyfriend was away again. He had a complicated life, always having to return to his country and help his family with money. He also worked, and they didn't have much time together.

He had seen this as an opportunity and taken it. Then there was a baby, so they stayed together for many years. He visited his family frequently and said he should go more often but didn't ask her to go with him. They didn't know her or their grandson, and he said she was busy with her career, and that was the excuse not to take her, so in some ways it was her fault, and some of what he said was true as she had taken on more as her sister's business grew. She had tried to reignite his interest, but it had not been enough. He then took his son to his family, making it seem acceptable, and he didn't notice details; her mother had always said to leave him to do what he wanted; once he would have done anything, but that had gone over the years, he had a good life, but it was not the life he wanted. The foreign boyfriend from years back had returned; she had thought maybe he had been the one there had been other relationships, one she had had another child with, the youngest grandchild. How many more would follow – she didn't want another child, but it remained to be seen.

She had a friendship with her Spanish business contact. He worked at the mill and convinced the mill owner to break away from tradition by employing him, and he met the mill owner's daughter and married her; everyone had things that were more important to them; to him, it was his career for her, it was wanting a partner to live at the house, having left and returned. Her meetings with him increased as her sister needed more fabric, and sometimes, with business completed, they would have a few drinks and talk, and they got on well. It could've been easy to have moved it from business, but Maisie didn't really want to upset other people, wanted something that would be for herself and his wife was a business contact who had brought wedding invitations for her own wedding and had recommended her to people that she knew, asked her sister to design and make her dress and bridesmaids' dresses. She was a friend of the family as well as a business contact and she should have loyalty from him – her father had given him a job and through that, he had a career and being married to the daughter had done very well at the mill. He always said that he never loved her as though it made his behaviour acceptable; he worked for her father, his wife had married him thinking that love would grow, but if it wasn't there in the beginning, it was unlikely that it would. Maisie could understand dependency could develop in a relationship; she had been dissatisfied with her relationship and her partner's reluctance to be with her at the house was another reason why she thought he had gone back to an old girlfriend, but to not know meant peace of mind but of course, it was there in her subconscious. She didn't have a reason to leave Chevelly House and the garden offered a place to reflect, to just sit and breathe the air and listen to the sounds and observe all the colours, the flowers and shrubs left to grow. It always looked different with the varying weather, the change in seasons. It was the garden that held them and even non-family members had sat there in bad times. Her mother said the house was not just bricks. It was memories, good and bad; it held them captive, but there would be a reason to leave the house in time.

CHAPTER THREE

LONDON BUSINESS

Beattie, her second daughter, was in her twenties and had dark hair and brown eyes. She had exceeded everybody's expectations, and definitely, those for herself, had achieved a dream for her designs to be in the Paris fashion houses there for a day years back with a man trying to impress her and decided that day her designs would be there. Her school uniforms where her career had started were the first choice for Scotland, with some success in England and Wales, but plaid or tartan wasn't appropriate there. She had successfully obtained orders from several schools for her jacket with short sleeves, which were her trademark plainer versions trimmed to add interest. She had not been to England before; when the headmaster of a school in London enquired about replacing their uniform, she decided to go to the school to talk to him and take Maisie, and she made arrangements. Marguerite took a few days off from the shop to look after the children, her grandson and two granddaughters.

They arrived in London. It was raining as they'd been told it mostly always was; she and Maisie with umbrellas – an aerial view would have shown an array of cascading colours as the umbrellas clicked shut one by one as the owners disappeared into the ground which housed the underground network. The school was a large private school; it was old and intimidating. It smelt musty as she pushed open the heavy door. There were a few students dressed in the school's colour which was green. In her head she was redressing them: tailored twill trousers, a long line jacket – her short-sleeved idea seemed less suitable here – a waistcoat, green and brown check, and yellow shirts. They reached reception, and while they waited she sketched with the coloured pencils she had in her bag. Maisie watched as in seconds in colour a boy and a girl materialised, the girl in a knee-length skirt, modern but not too tight as freedom of movement was a feature of her designs, as were light materials – expensive but machine washable – a yellow shirt with a waistcoat, long socks in yellow.

She turned to speak: "They'll prefer to keep white or grey." She had a supplier already but perhaps this time they'd take the yellow option.

Maisie nodded; the boy in tailored trousers with a shirt, a waistcoat which could be worn with a long line coat.

Twenty minutes later they were called in. Had Beattie thought ahead and had other ideas?

"No," she said – didn't know until she had got here.

They were offered coffee or tea served from a push along trolley. The headmaster was about fifty with greying hair and had tiny spectacles perched on the end of his nose, washed out blue eyes which looked at the girls who were dripping water. "Yes, that's London, always raining, well so often that's how you thought of it, ladies. This is a girl thing, isn't it?" He called over his secretary, a dowdy looking lady. "What do you think?" He showed her Beattie's designs.

"Very nice," she said. "May I make a suggestion though? Jumpers, cardigans for those cold days – it's a draughty old building."

She smiled. They were old fashioned and could be bought, not designed, but she quickly sketched an old fashioned style sleeveless jumper; it was brown, green, old leather. Perhaps the girls could have the waistcoats they liked, the long line jackets for both girls and boys. The items would have to be made before a decision could be reached and this was an area where you could win or lose – the interest was there, the actual value of the potential order was high as it was a private school, and money was no object.

He said, "You're a clever girl," peering again over his spectacles and said, "you are still young."

Maisie asked about the school and its history. The headmaster was always happy to talk about his school's achievements and said he would talk to the governors. "Pleased to meet you, girls." He stood and shook their hands.

The secretary smiled; she had enjoyed being asked her opinion on such an important part of school matters. They said they'd be back when they had the clothes available, and it would take a while. The headmaster nodded. Outside, it was still raining, their umbrellas up. They got on a double-decker bus that had just stopped. They didn't know where it was going, but it got them out of the rain.

She had some of her work in Europe but not uniforms. There was a lot to consider, so for now, this part of her business had gone as far as it could. There were new students every year, and replacing worn and grown out of uniforms bought in an income, and it didn't need much of her time. She was designing party and dance dresses for girls and formal outfits for boys, and hats, and she had moved to her mother's shop. With some training, the assistant was able to decorate them, keeping the Beattie design label. Her dresses were her main interest for the wealthy Scottish and the aristocracy. It was not easy to keep them original. She had been asked years ago by Lady Asher to make a dress for her daughter for an occasion. The girl said she liked ballet and another dress was made. This had given her daughter, a quiet child, a lot of attention, and dance outfits had become another part of her business. Lady Asher was now a family friend, they were always on the guest list for parties and asked to call for a drink in the better weather and sit outside on the terrace. This connection had brought business from people within that circle, and when it was possible Elodie was with her. She had made a dress for Lady Asher, which she had been very pleased with, and it had been made by a child, which she was then, and her business had increased. She now designed dresses for formal occasions and parties for Lady Asher, her associates and friends. She was now very wealthy but it was the expression on her clients' faces when they opened the boxes. She could easily afford a home of her own, but her home was Chevelly House and she put her money into her savings – the loan that included buying the shop had been paid off; now the house was the only home they and their children had known. It may not have been traditional but it worked for them; over the years it had ruined all their relationships, not wanting to leave, and she had now paid her father his part of the cost of the house. She and her boyfriend had been in and out of each other's lives for years; he could've fitted in at Chevelly House, he had always been confident in himself, unthreatened by successful women; she didn't want another child but he thought he would in time. He was the brother of her sister's boyfriend, and she was sure he knew what his brother was doing but never mentioned the visits and the messages stopped. They needed to be free. He was the uncle of her nephew, he'd been part of their lives; he'd helped her by sending photos of her designs to a magazine. She was not even 30. The businesses were growing, and her ability to control it. Not wanting to be in an advisory role, she had become successful at a young age. Where could she go from here?

Frankie, her eldest son, had eventually given vent to years of resentment, leaving nothing out. He was a boy who needed a role model – his father had tried to rectify this in later years. He could not deal with him, he avoided conflict and had not spoken to him for years. He had also lost his younger son, loyal to his brother, and Frankie had gone feral.

CHAPTER FOUR

CONSEQUENCES

It started with him playing truant for a day here and there; he left for school with his brother but then made an excuse to stay outside the gates while his brother went in. He had told her when she said the school had phoned to make her aware. He was angry, couldn't explain, hated school, and had no idea what he could do. He wasn't clever. What was he interested in, she asked.

"Nothing!" he shouted, and then said he liked cars.

"That's an interest. Perhaps you could be a mechanic."

"Maybe," he said. He had sat defeated, his shoulders slumped.

She recalled how Beattie had been at a similar age. You outgrew school before it did you. He was not academic and found authority difficult. He was always picking up and dropping girlfriends, had a rangy build, all arms and legs, sharp features and very dark eyes that looked like trouble and had a personality to match. Marguerite was always understanding, trying to find ways to help, and arranged boxing to help with his anger. This appeared to be the turning point in his aggressiveness, making him more rather than less, and his younger brother also wanted to have lessons. He turned out to be the better fighter with the right attitude, understanding it was a skill, not an opportunity to hurt someone, and he'd achieved success in the sport. Frankie used to be the one in the lead and fell behind, and he didn't like this; idle hands find the devil's work, don't they?

"So let's try to concentrate on being a mechanic, but you must finish school. It's the law."

He said he would, and for a few weeks, he went to school, but something in him longed for excitement.

Marguerite considered how their lives had been so settled until she and her husband split. Frankie and her youngest son's lives diversified, events they could not believe started to happen and socialising outside the usual circles brought trouble to the house. Frankie had got involved with other boys looking for a fun life in the village. It was uneventful; his younger brother had gone with him until he had been taken up with his sport and didn't have the time, and Frankie, used to having him to look out for, felt lost. It had been his role. Without him, there was no reason for caution. He needed to find an outlet.

The police had again become part of their lives. Frankie's interest in cars had led him to steal them while driving illegally; Beattie wanted to help by suggesting driving lessons and buying him a car, but he'd said he wanted to be able to buy his own.

Meanwhile, he would steal them. He liked to drive, but the excitement and risk that was part of it made him and a friend drive them. They'd joyride them, and then they'd dump them. Not thinking he was clever, he had the mind to work out how to dismantle alarms and get into the cars. It seemed he was cleverer than he thought.

The night he had been caught and taken to the police station, he was alone. His friend had lost his nerve. Beattie released him on bail, and she had defended him as a character reference in court. He narrowly escaped being locked away and was given a suspended sentence. Even then his father had not talked to his son, he had not mastered the understanding of people's flaws and not those of his child.

CHAPTER FIVE

ARRANGEMENTS

Christmas was now approaching. Frankie was in prison; driving and stealing cars had been addictive, but at least now they didn't have to worry about the police knocking on the door.

The shop was busy with shoppers for gifts, but her assistant noticed Marguerite was subdued and not in the mood for Christmas this year. Malvina assured her she could close the shop and said she should go home, so she got in her car and found her mind going back to other Christmases when all the family had been there. She arrived at Chevelly House and opened the door. It still creaked and had for years, a job that never got done. It needed oil. She could hear the family. It had felt wrong without Frankie, but at the same time, not having to worry about where he was or, worse, what he was doing, was a relief.

They now owned the house. Beattie had been able to pay the half that wasn't hers, and she only had to pay the bills. She went into the lounge, opened the patio doors, went outside and lit a cigarette, her thoughts again returning to other Christmases.

Roly had moved out of his rented apartment and bought a small house with the money he had got from the house. There was room enough for visitors, though he had never been interested in that, and his girlfriend hadn't moved into the house, and, although divorced, he didn't want to remarry. Marguerite thought that his girlfriend

Verity had a choice, didn't she, and had chosen to wait; marriage was outdated it seemed these days for the younger generations; the older ones who tried it once didn't want to marry again.

This year, Maisie had invited Esmeralda's father to be at the house; he was a Scottish man, a man whom even her father accepted, and that children out of wedlock were commonplace, had acted appropriately, congratulating her on her second child, a girl Esmeralda, another blonde child – none of the dark genes had come through in the grandchildren. Esmeralda had pure white poker straight hair, a small face with large brown eyes, and a tiny little rosebud mouth like a doll and was a demanding child. Maisie had tired of a volatile partner and the relationship with Esmeralda's dad continued, but her reluctance to leave the house, and that her children, a boy and a girl, would not have their own rooms if it was a two bedroom house, the reason not to have a permanent relationship with him. He was not in a position to buy a bigger house but it was a convenient excuse as she had no intention of leaving Chevelly House. Marguerite thought it was up to him to work out a way.

It was a long journey to England, where his father lived, so Colm would be at the house. In past years, Elodie had sometimes gone to her father's, and Beattie had too, but now, she thought portraying them as a family was wrong. Yes, they were, but he wasn't her partner. Elodie was here and would be at her dad's the next day.

Maurice was bringing his girlfriend. He was now a successful boxer. He stayed with a girl and usually took a while to decide; he would treat them well when he did – a houseful of mostly women had taught him a lot. The girlfriend was very quiet and seemed lacking in personality, but Marguerite could understand it was hard to rise above all the strong personalities in the house. She was maybe quietly confident and would be at the house and liked her son.

14

Beattie, having to talk with people most of the time, was happy to be at the house with just her family and said to her mother that she didn't have anyone important enough to invite for the day after it had ended with her mother's younger partner as they expected it to at some point. She suspected his family had pressured him to get away, she had met a few men since but none she wanted to settle with, so was alone for now. Busy with supporting Beattie with her career and with Frankie she visited him regularly, Beattie said she would go but he said no. His mother brought cigarettes and chocolate, sweets and other things that he sometimes gave to others, he was with people who had made mistakes and he didn't want to have to think about how his life had been before. Roly had found it difficult with what had happened to his daughters and couldn't accept and understand how a boy from a privileged family had fallen to this, where had they gone wrong. Marguerite had found herself thinking often had he not got what he needed as a child though anyone would say looking in he had it all and somehow this had distorted his way of thinking. Remembering she longed to have something to fight for and that in Frankie it had come out in a wrong way, he didn't care about consequences, didn't think they'd happen – he explained about the cars, he hadn't meant to steal them, he just hadn't been able to resist the overwhelming desire to be behind the wheel of an expensive car. Driving at speed he felt alive; just one wouldn't have ever been enough. He was alright, he didn't actually like prison, but there he was safe from himself. Marguerite understood and hoped he could have a normal life outside one day but for now this was his life.

CHAPTER SIX

FREEDOM LOST

He had been given a two-year sentence, broken his suspended sentence, which involved meetings with a probation officer; it was a waste of time; in his opinion his cravings to be behind the wheel were so intense he could taste it but he didn't voice this. The counsellor assigned was languishing quietly, looking unthreatening, waiting for him to unburden himself, but he didn't want to do that and sat in silence and gave absolutely nothing away, lost in his own place. The meetings stopped; all he could think of was how for a while the adrenaline had kicked in, and he felt alive sitting behind the wheel, driving a stolen car, always prestigious, top of the range, and he had no choice but to give in to this. He thought his skills on immobilising alarms perfect, but he had made that one mistake and was now locked up with angry people, betrayed usually by a woman, some just the thrill of theft but getting rid of stolen goods wasn't easy and this had led to them being found out, arrested, then locked away. Drug dealers also make mistakes, even the ones that had thought of all the possibilities. He couldn't quite believe it when he had been at dinner one evening and there was a familiar face sat at a table; they were in long lines, in a room accommodating half the prisoners at one sitting, the other half at a later one. You couldn't choose; you ate whether you were hungry or liked the food, you were discriminating at the start but you learnt that if you didn't eat it was a long time until breakfast. He always had food he could eat, but ate to keep his strength up – you didn't need to risk weakness, someone might decide they didn't like you and to be faced with a strong stare, not someone who was hungry from lack of food was the better option.

He was young but not the youngest; there were boys under twenty, and it was hard for them but some of them looked like proper hardened criminals; he could not have thought that someone like him would be here and how far he had fallen. But he got wise and knew who not to talk to, and who would want to speak to him. He looked again at the man opposite him – where had he seen him? Yes, it had been at Beattie's sixteenth birthday; he wouldn't want him to remember him, he was a child then and it was a long time ago. This man was in his thirties possibly, had black hair and tattoos, was hard faced, no eye contact was made, and he did what he could to avoid him. He spent a lot of time in his cell and chose to spend more, he had to go for the daily walk outside; he missed the house amongst a lot of other things, and the garden – it was a concrete area in the yard. He and some of the inmates would kick a ball around. He'd always liked football. Fortunately, there was no sign of this man. Like with meals, they were told when they could go out and their times didn't coincide. In the evenings they could watch TV, play board games, or just talk. Concerned that this man would remember him, he didn't go to the room. It was one less thing he could do in this limited environment but he was sure that he could appear at any time, so he escaped confrontation and why would there have been any – this man had played a part in their lives but he didn't remember, he feared him but didn't know why. He tried to think of earlier memories but there had been so much change in his life when he had been young, it was difficult to put them in place. He had no choice – his cell was the only place where you could be alone. It was grim and smelt of disinfectant, but he was forced into the company of these men; some appeared to be sociable, they picked on loners, weren't they all the same – no one was allowed to think they were better or more important than anyone else – but the level of crimes were as varied as the characters. Some were nice – how had they got here? Some shared stories; the ones that didn't he understood were there for the worst crimes.

He was the one who always had something to give to the others, little things, soap that smelt nice, and shampoo, and he shared with those who had tired of the stench that followed them and others – it was fear. If he was soft when he arrived, daily he became less so, hardened over time; he was not the man he came in as and didn't know if he could go back to his former life. Of course, he was Frankie, but they wouldn't know him, not that they had understood him before – and how could they? He didn't understand himself. But that could be a good thing. They had not liked what he had become.

He stayed in his cell, reading any magazines or books his mother brought in, furthering his knowledge of the mechanics of cars, looking at the photos, determined to overcome his problem of being able to understand letters and numbers which were the foundation of any career. He knew it would be difficult on the outside, but his knowledge would persuade some employer to give him a chance.

There was a knock on the door. That usually only happened when he got a call, but it wasn't – it was a letter. Though he did get a letter sometimes, he didn't like news from outside, there wasn't anything he could do in here and he couldn't get away from his thoughts. It was a letter from Lady Asher's daughter. They were friends; they had met at social events at the castle. Her mother wouldn't be pleased that she had decided to write to Frankie. She had improved in appearance over the years, had always seemed to like him, but Frankie had never thought of her as a possible girlfriend – she was hardly his type. She had written to him but he wasn't a letter writer and he struggled with the words, but was determined and he had improved and was good at the spoken word, which had got him into trouble, but he was fine with that now. He wrote back – what did he have to lose? He had plenty of time, considered each word; the spelling was hard but after several attempts the letter was good enough to be sent. The letters were vetted, more so those that came in, but it gave him something to do, and it developed and a kind of feeling the thief and the genteel – it was an unlikely match. She liked him, she said, why he thought he was good looking he had been told. She had sent a photo which he stuck on the wall. She was someone outside the family; had he not become a criminal her parents could possibly have thought him suitable for their daughter – he was from a wealthy family, after all. She continued with the letters and they increased in frequency. It was a good way to get to know a person.

After eighteen months he was released early for good behaviour. She had given him something to think about and made him feel hopeful. He was grateful to her but he didn't want her or anyone else to be there on the day. He looked around his cell to make sure he hadn't forgotten anything. There hadn't been much time after he was convicted to think what he would need; he had never been in prison before. The cell had to be empty. He put everything into a bag, and walked to the gates. Two guards were stood there; they spoke to him. He had not been a troublemaker inside, he was very careful. He had been friendly with everyone, but too suspicious to trust anyone fully; they were not his friends now. On his final day when papers for his release were handed to him, they told him to stay away and not keep contact, he could now start again and that he had a girlfriend. One of the guards unlocked the gate and when he walked out locked it again. He walked to the bus stop. He didn't have to wait long – a few minutes later the bus arrived and he got on and sat thinking. He thought of Prunella and that

Lady Asher had liked him previously and he had been to the castle on several occasions, but how would she think of him now? He recalled how she refused her daughter nothing. He wouldn't want to cause problems with his sisters' contacts and association with the family, it was up to the girl not him.

He needed his first few hours outside to be alone to think about how he felt about being back with his family and how they would be with him. It was now a reality, not just a far-off thought of a day that felt like it would never arrive. He was anxious away from his cell but he concentrated on what he would do. He had some money as they were given work in the prison, but he didn't need to buy anything, so he'd not used it. He didn't have a problem with drugs that had been and getting caught and locked away probably saved him from possibly worse, finding himself taking stronger drugs to remove himself from what he considered he couldn't deal with. Very few people would understand how he who had so much as a boy, had got himself in this situation, and smoking was allowed in the prison – even the non-smokers on the outside became smokers inside as they could not get drugs. He suspected there were ways. His mother bought him cigarettes or tobacco so didn't have to pay for them and he would give them to others if they had run out. He was sure that they were able to get drugs, but had not wanted to know, and if questioned he could honestly say that he didn't. He had gone to the gym most days and his body was now muscular; his hair was very short, which had been compulsory. His mother had brought him a tailored suit, a slimline cotton shirt, a tie and shoes. He had concentrated daily on getting through; the shoes were hard on his feet as he wore trainers and the prison clothes were loose but with everything new he was a new man. He was cleanly shaven, and sprayed aftershave, and gelled his hair. He looked good and wanted to start over. He had been told his record would stay with him; he had contacts outside but wouldn't talk to any of them.

Beattie would give him an opportunity if he allowed her to – she was wealthy and well known. He had heard nothing from his father, he still couldn't face the truth that they all had flaws. He knew that he wouldn't go to his father until he could be good at something. He had a girlfriend – would she be at the house? He'd mentioned her to his mother, and she could sense trouble. They had known each other as children but too different to be in a relationship. He walked from the bus stop and arrived at the house. He had been away for eighteen months and hadn't thought of this day but after being inside, he had conflicting feelings about being back. He would not have the routine that had kept him busy on the inside, and how would they be with him, would they be pleased he was back?

The cars – his mother's, Maisie's, Beattie's and Maurice's – he matched them to their owners, and he reminded himself the next car he drove would be his own. He rang the bell and the first person he saw was Maurice – who would have been the person his brother would most want to see before the others. He looked familiar, his hair was quite long – it suited him. There was a time when haircuts were an unnecessary expense and they'd both had hair on their collars. Was he still boxing, he asked him. "Yes," he said. He'd written to him after he'd had come to terms with what had happened. He knew the real Frankie, it was just general things without drawing his attention to what he'd thrown away. Frankie felt ill at ease. Maurice said he was pleased he was back – they'd never been apart until Frankie was sent away – but Frankie looked close to tears. He wanted to turn round and walk out, he felt like he didn't have a place in the house and everyone would be concerned at what he might do now.

"Let's get a drink," Maurice said.

He noticed he now had a confidence, he was placid but strong – his little brother had gone on to be well known in the boxing field. He was with a girl in jeans and a shirt; she looked like a quiet girl. He noticed her little hands and old trainers. She was smiling at him, meeting his eyes. There may be more to her than first appeared. She didn't seem to be scared of him – what had Maurice said about him? He went into the lounge. A 'welcome home' banner stretched across the length of the room, the family were all there. He was moved and struggled to look pleased to be back, but felt out of place after his little cell. His mother looked pleased but he knew she would be thinking would he, but he wouldn't, he'd try not to.

"Well look at you," she said.

He looked anything but a man who'd been in prison. All eyes were on him while they took in that he was standing in the room. Maisie and Beattie rushed over and hugged him, the children looking at him thinking who was he but knowing this man looked familiar but all dressed up. They were in clothes to sit around in. The smallest one would not recall him; she stared at him and he smiled. They had noticeably grown. He'd been out of their lives for eighteen months; children forget. But, they welcomed him in their way, giving hugs as if expected. It was a party, but the air was filled with something intangible – he got it, he's back, he knew how much trouble he had caused.

Later on the doorbell rang. "For you?" his mother said. Was it his dad – he couldn't deal with that. He went and opened the door, and there she was, slim and delicate, her large eyes looking up at him. She held her arms out to him; he was home. He had known her for years but not as a girlfriend.

"Hello Frankie." She smiled and kissed his lips. He could've left with her then. Was he in love? He didn't know what to say so he put his arm around her and his eyes fell to her feet. She wore light blue ballet style shoes – she was a ballet dancer, nicely dressed and slim; she wasn't his type at all and from an upper class background. He was from a well-known respected family though they were perhaps not that now – any idea he was better than anyone had been knocked out of him with the daily grind of prison life. He was reluctant to act on any feelings but didn't want to have negative thoughts and he couldn't change what had happened to him. She had driven from the castle in a silver Mercedes sports car. It was parked with the other cars. Beads of sweat starting to break out – had he got over his problem? Any of these cars he could drive if allowed; he would have to take a driving test but that should not be a problem. But he was getting ahead of himself.

She was watching him. He felt tense but he needed to get away, he couldn't cope. She understood and said to take some time and he left her with his family. His mother followed him out and closed the door and all the pent up emotion, holding his breath, being careful in all ways what he said, who he spoke to, it all just flowed out of him. He sobbed; any joy and excitement was gone. He couldn't cope and went to his room, unable to face anyone; but sitting in his room was not unlike what he had been used to, although his room was clean with new curtains and bedcovers and a rug. He sat on his bed. He didn't know how to feel or what to do; he was exhausted. His last eighteen months had been easy in the sense it had been to get through. Here it wasn't raw. He dealt better with that. He needed to get out, find a gym, perhaps get outside to walk and that he could now go anywhere was at the front of his mind. Prunella was downstairs, but how could she or any of them understand? It all seemed difficult – he wasn't just going to live happily ever after.

A tap on the door pulled him out from his mental turmoil. It was Beattie. She said it was a shock to be home and he had more important things to consider, just adjusting was enough. "We shouldn't have asked her but she didn't want to wait. It is easy to just fall into something," she said, meaning Prunella.

He was choked with feelings and that they seemed so strong. "Don't know," he said.

"She's a daughter of a Lord and Lady and you're now an ex-con."

He knew he was and he felt he was not entitled to even think of himself as a boyfriend for her now, an unlikely choice for anything, but he couldn't think in that way, there would be time for that later. She was right: Prunella had waited eighteen months or longer for all he knew; there was no hurry.

She handed him a box. "You'll need this." And she left.

He opened it: a mobile phone. He hadn't wanted handouts but to Beattie it wasn't. She would say he needed a phone and she could afford it. He felt a failure. He needed to go back downstairs. The party was for him. Prunella, everyone knew her – even Maurice's girlfriend whom he'd met a year ago. He expected there had been events at the castle and she had been taken and introduced. It seemed serious between them with her next to him looking confident. After prison life the surroundings seemed bright, everything was grey inside or beige. He was aware of the trappings of money here; could he adjust? He felt he would be comfortable in a bedsit but he knew that in his finery he looked right here, he would be alright. The time inside had cleared his head. He would need a while to adjust. He thought it wasn't the time to be considering what next, it was a moment in time he would not forget. He'd been given another chance. He wouldn't waste it.

Later, champagne glasses that had been dusted were brought out. They stood up and all went round clinking their glasses. Colm and Elodie were pleased at being able to join the toast, Esmeralda waved her glass, spilling the little bit she had been allowed. "To Frankie." They were complete, all family members present, Maisie, Beattie and Mum with no men in their lives – those places were yet to be filled.

CHAPTER SEVEN

HOME

It wasn't just a case of you're out now and going back to your former life. He couldn't do that or return to his life before the trouble started. He could only go forward. It was like before, when nobody commented on his behaviour. He felt like an imposter dressed in his finery, like it was a disguise, and he didn't yet deserve the look. Any idea he was anything other than a man who had been to prison had been knocked out of him. He was not someone to be admired or respected, like his family, who were all achievers. He was reluctant to continue on the path he found himself on with her, thinking they were in a relationship when he could already foresee the outcome. He didn't want pressure or to have negative thoughts, but how could he judge his true feelings? It wasn't normal circumstances.

She had driven from the castle in a silver Mercedes sports car – it would likely have been a present, not bought with her own money. She didn't work – they didn't – and how they got money he didn't know. They had events, but the way they lived with all the staff that would certainly cost a lot. She would have an allowance – all rich children got that. She was a small girl, her eyes taking over her thin face. He was not a good idea for her, not yet, she was out of place and definitely out of time in his life; he had been locked away, he couldn't deal with her. Her car looked wrong next to his brother and sisters', symbols of their success, which they had paid for with their own money; his mum's car was used for her work and to take her grandchildren out, taking over the places where they had all sat at different times. Her car represented her status as the daughter of aristocratic parents. She wasn't a girl from the village a day ago; he was in prison; he'd got used to that life and had a routine. Making decisions made his head hurt. The cars were a glaring reminder – had he got over his problem? These cars he could drive with a licence and the owner's permission, but he wanted his own. He felt that a relationship with her would be a secret on her side; she hadn't mentioned her parents, and he hadn't asked. But he was getting ahead of himself – she wasn't saying anything, but he already felt attached, or was it just that he'd had little contact with anyone for so long? She understood his reluctance and said there was no rush and to call when he was ready. Their lips had touched. He'd wanted to hug and kiss her, release all the tension, but he knew he must not. He would call of course, and "thank you for everything" – that hadn't sounded like himself talking. She smiled then he didn't want to feel responsible for her feelings and she left. He had gone back into the house.

The family was busy and gave Frankie time. He was in his room, replacing one prison with another; in his room, everything was clean. The last eighteen months he thought had been easier when he had a routine, a daily workout at the gym. The days and nights in his cell were long, but every day was one less here. It wasn't raw. He coped better with that. He needed to get outside. At the forefront of his mind was Prunella. He could arrive at her door, but you didn't at the castle. He would need to have been invited or to have asked in advance. He was an ex-con and would not just live happily ever after.

There was a knock on the door It was Beattie. "Morning," she said as though it was just another day. She sat on the chair next to his bed. "You like cars." It was a dangerous topic. "You need to learn to drive."

He could; he had to be able to drive legally and it was the first thing he would do, or he would stay in his room. He had got over his drug addiction, and it wasn't mentioned. He shouldn't be getting involved with Prunella and was it because she had reached out to him? He was unsure. Beattie kept work and relationships separate. She had helped him, but he had a lot to do before he would be ready for anything and he needed time to adjust; his mother would say that everything finds its way. He set up his phone, and it didn't take very long, and then he thought of Prunella. He messaged 'good morning' and she replied but he didn't message again. He could start today. He had some money, so he could pay for one lesson. He didn't want to be given the money; he knew he had to continue pushing himself. He didn't want it to be easy. His family had money, so he wouldn't have to pay for anything; but he wasn't going to fall into that trap.

His family were in the kitchen and his mum had booked a week's holiday. He felt himself relaxing; nobody said anything in particular to him, just talked amongst themselves. The children had a day off, an Inset day, and they would be back at school tomorrow.

Colm asked if he wanted to go to the garden to play basketball. Yes, he said, and the garden welcomed him back. The children were good company, and it was fun. Esmeralda was trying to get the ball through the hoop. He picked her up, and she put the ball through; Colm and Elodie were laughing and said that it was cheating. The time flew. He had been aware of every minute inside and didn't want to return there.

He was in the passenger seat of the car. He felt calm. The driving instructor was behind the wheel and went over the basics; most of the lesson was taken up with this part. When he was able to drive, he effortlessly pulled away onto the road, left then right, then a roundabout. He could drive; the instructor said he didn't need lessons and told him to apply for his test – there was nothing he could teach him. He would need to know the theory and he could use his car for the test. He took his mobile number and said he'd call him and let him know when there was a test available. Before all his problems, he'd always been confident. Until the secondary school had become aware that he had difficulties with letters but that was the past; now he needed to earn money, he would need a car. Beattie said he could work on the extension. When it was complete she would buy him a car to the value of the work – he would earn it, she said. Yes he would, he said.

Maurice trained daily at the gym or ran locally or in the mountains, boxing some weekends. He wasn't fully employed, but he earned enough. He didn't have a house to pay for or maintain; he contributed to Chevelly House. Frankie went running with him. Maurice said maybe he could go boxing again. He didn't want to do that for many reasons and said no, so they ran daily regardless of the weather and didn't discuss the past.

Roly's son was out of prison; Verity had been supportive and said that his family were all characters and that he found it difficult to accept the complicated factors that made a person, they were talented. Had all that come from Marguerite; her talent was family, taking the punches and modifying the fallout, and she had her own business. Verity suited him; she liked a quiet life and wanted to live with him and be his wife. He was so set in his ways, refusing to understand anything or anyone. Sometimes she thought she should leave, she uncharacteristically attacked him, verbally annoyed at the lack of progress. It was such a waste, she said, a big family but he didn't appreciate them. She had one daughter from a previous marriage. Roly let her leave, he didn't call. How did he feel about Verity? He left it a month, wanting to know if he would miss her and that he didn't understand women, but he should. Would she move on and find a man ready to join her in a proper life and theirs was not? Days and then weeks went by but she made no contact, his life empty again. He hadn't progressed at work, he had lost his ambition that was linked to the house, that had represented his success, the holidays and his children, but that had long gone now, he had nothing, no reason. Marguerite's life was busy as was the house as none of the children had left. She had split a long time ago with her younger partner and now they were both without someone. It hadn't been confirmed that his relationship had ended. She in her way had given an ultimatum. They had got along. Marguerite would never settle for that. He picked up his phone. She was surprised to hear from him and he asked about each of the children, even the grandchildren. She was not convinced, though. "They are all fine," she replied, thinking Frankie was the reason for the call; she thought it had been Verity who had said that he should call. Frankie, he had messed up very badly, but he was their son, he was sorry, he couldn't help it. "Help it then," she said. She put the phone down but as a gesture she sent him Frankie's mobile number. "Up to you now," the message said. She could not stand in the way of a reconciliation – her son would need it, anything that helped him feel better about himself. Frankie had been busy on the extension, had taken his theory test, and had booked the driving test.

He had been in contact with Prunella, messaging, but the protection of not being able to meet had made it unreal now. There was no reason why they shouldn't be together other than he didn't want to be a secret perhaps – she had called to the house, they were all there, he didn't know if she had told her mother, had said nothing about parents. He didn't take her to his room. Everyone's eyes were on them. He received a call from an unrecognised number, but the voice he did recognise.

"Frankie, I would like to talk."

"Yes," he replied.

His car appeared later that evening. On hearing the roar of the engine Frankie went out. His dad was in the passenger seat and he handed him the keys. Frankie felt the adrenaline, he pulled onto the road. His dad put back the sunroof, it was a bit cold. Common ground had been found, they didn't talk, it was just the sound of the engine. A while later they returned and Frankie put aside all that had happened. He said, "Come in for a coffee." They walked together into the house. Marguerite was in the kitchen; she had coffee made. She poured two more then she picked up her cup and said, "I'll leave you to talk," and went to the lounge. The patio doors were as usual open; she lit a cigarette and sat outside.

Roly had been surprised – but then should he have been – at how well he could drive. He recalled how excited as a boy Frankie had been about cars, then his time as a car thief and they'd only been expensive cars. It had been like a drug. Roly hoped that this was now over. He had heard through a business contact that the company had recently lost a chauffeur, and knew his son would have no problem with the test. He called and mentioned Frankie, giving brief details, and he left it to the company to decide. Maurice messaged with one word thanks; with that one word he left a window open for him; he had not had much contact with them, they were adults now; he was getting old and didn't want to waste any more time. He could retire. He had considered it recently but retired with Verity – she was a bit younger though, she could decide to but she liked her work. She knew he wouldn't want her company all the time and he wouldn't want to start over again with somebody, but not marriage; she could move in. He called her. "Yes?" she answered and he felt that a rejection was about to be given. "Would you still like to live with me?" She didn't respond immediately. Was she crying? "Are you sure?" convinced that he could've changed his mind. "Yes," he replied.

Frankie received a message; it was from Mr Spirros. "Hello Frankie, your dad says you're looking for a job, was this right? He says you are a good driver. I have a fleet of cars and need a new chauffeur for myself and other colleagues. Let me know as soon as possible, Spirrosindustries.co.uk". He had not thought he'd get a job and to be recommended by his dad. He was careful to spell correctly as he tapped out a message, although the phone alerted him on spelling mistakes. It also had a calculator, so numbers were less of an issue. His driving test was soon. If he kept to the speed limit, he would have no problem. He confirmed his interest, time, and place, and yes, thank you, sir; this was an opportunity. He couldn't fail the test. It could all fall into place. Everything always does; his mother would say he just had to be patient. He didn't want to tell anyone; he had the suit so he could wear that. Nobody took much notice of what he was doing; all the family were occupied with their own agenda, and that was how they were in his family. Nobody was aware of what any of the others were doing. He was working on the extension and could be missed, but the rain had stopped any work today so he could go without anyone noticing he wasn't there.

Two hours before the test, which was standard procedure, the driving instructor would go over a few things and practise any weaknesses. By the time the test was due, the rain had almost stopped. He couldn't make any mistakes; he could drive but had to keep to the speed limit and exaggerate movements, but ultimately, he was to drive; reversing, he was very good at that. Having backed up stolen cars... he tried not to think of his record. Would he have to say anything about his past? He hoped this man would respect his dad's judgement, but his mind needed to stay focused. He listened to the instructions in the driving seat, and the test went well. The window wipers worked hard as the rain started with a vengeance. He arrived back at the driving school and went in. The examiner and the instructor shook his hand. "Well done, boy," he said.

On his return to the house, he got a few snacks and a beer from the empty kitchen, then went to his room. They rarely ate together. When Mum's man had cooked they had then, though Mum did insist on a Sunday meal together, and Beattie and Elodie would cook. Two days later he got ready for the interview. He was dressed in his suit, and he had a taxi booked. Everyone was a bit careful with him; Mum commented and waited for an explanation, but he didn't want to say anything. Beattie had gone out early with Elodie, and Colm was getting ready for school.

Esmeralda was bouncing around, bright and energetic. "You look nice, Frankie," she said, her tiny little mouth smiling sweetly, but that could change when she couldn't get her way.

He thanked her and she was then off after her mother. It was a nice day to be in the garden and Maisie had her laptop. He didn't see Maurice. He got in the taxi – the driver was their friend who only did the occasional pick up these days. He had to tell someone; he said that it was something good at last. He was a nice man, non-judgemental and well thought of by them all.

He arrived at the large office block. He took the lift to the fourth floor. The doors opened onto an open office area with some closed doors, one with gold lettering with the name Andreous Spirros. Frankie knocked and felt a slight surge of nerves, which he fought away. A small bald man got up from behind a desk; Frankie towered over him and held out his hand. It was shaken with a surprisingly firm grip. Mr Spirros smiled; he had a missing tooth. He spoke in broken English with an accent using some Greek words. Frankie didn't know much about the business. His search had revealed nothing. He didn't care; the policy of not knowing worked well for him. Mr Spirros said they were international so he would have to travel and there would be driving to the airport and other places; he would sometimes have to wait around but he was used to waiting. He didn't say why. It was a good job. He told him how much he would get paid; he could drive, that was what he wanted to do, he wasn't overly concerned about details and his potential boss wasn't and didn't ask him anything about what he wanted or had done before – Frankie would be suitable for the job. Mr Spirros saw a young, well-dressed man from a wealthy family, not an ex-con. He would be expected to drive any of the cars at any time and be available at unsociable hours. He would be given a car today, the job was his, no call-back in a few days, tomorrow he had to drive Mr Spirros to a meeting in Edinburgh. He handed him a set of keys and they got the lift to the ground floor, then there were stairs to an area below where a row of cars were parked, all high prestige. He felt the adrenaline surface. His key opened a red Jaguar. His mouth was dry. He could legally drive this car! He couldn't hide his excitement.

Mr Spirros noticed. "You like the car? Be outside the office at ten."

Had his father said anything about his crimes? He, a car thief, was now in possession of a very valuable car – but he wasn't that person anymore. The car quietly glided; it had a very gentle roar. It smelt of leather and was spotless inside – he would keep it that way, that was part of what was expected of him, always to be smartly dressed and the car immaculate. His confidence levels soared – he didn't feel like the old Frankie Chevelly, he felt like a new one.

CHAPTER EIGHT

NEWCOMER

Work had started on the new playroom/bedroom. It was outside the house, so there would be minimum disruption to the inside. All the boys were involved in the work; it wasn't a question of money, but they didn't like strangers or trust them. They needed someone with real expertise to oversee the project. It was Maisie who had found him. He had put in a new bathroom at the castle, keeping in style with a claw foot bath with varied but suitable furnishings. The overall effect was like stepping into the past. It was a professional ensuite to the main bedroom, and he was multiskilled. He was right for them and the extension.

The relationship with Esmeralda's dad lacked excitement, which Maisie had previously thought she didn't need anymore. He was generous and gave a lot of attention to both her and his child, but she was now interested in the builder; perhaps he was resigned and probably didn't know how he'd got with her at all, and possibly all her past conquests had thought this as the years went by. She had not had any intention of moving in with him – he was not able to afford to buy a larger house with separate rooms for the children, a reason she had given. Perhaps he would be relieved nobody noticed he wasn't around as much other than Marguerite, who could see that Maisie was about to let go of any control. It would be the end of yet another relationship; Brodie, he'd not made an impression on them. But they liked him, even their father; it seemed Maisie was wrong. Brodie had hidden depths and wasn't just going to be kicked away; he knew that Maisie was considering ending the relationship, he could feel it and said he wanted to discuss Esmeralda. "Why?" she asked. He didn't want to talk on the phone, she hadn't finished with him and they were parents to Esmeralda so she agreed to meet with him.

The builder had a Scottish accent, and he had lived in Scotland for years, but there was something foreign about him. She later discovered that he had Scottish grandparents, his mother had married a Polish man, he was unexpectedly tall considering his ancestry and taller than Maisie, even with her heels so they were suited by appearance. Maisie liked to wear heels, and Greg had never looked quite right with her, but he had tried, yet he'd tired of not receiving the same in return. She had heard that he was in a relationship, but information about her remained unknown. She would not want to know and what did it matter, she'd moved on with Brodie and she now looked as though she was moving on again. Brodie looked respectable. He was a bit shorter than her. He was a man who considered family important, but Maisie found there was chemistry with the builder; he looked like a player, but even players eventually fall. Maisie was more herself; in a way, it was nice to see, but they felt a bit sorry for Brodie. It wouldn't affect Esmeralda. She would still go to him and stay a weekend, which could work well for Maisie.

Beattie had successfully got the contract for the London school uniform and she and Maisie returned for a visit to show the uniforms. She had since taken on a building where the uniforms were made, employed a team of workers to ensure they were made to the highest standard, and paid them well. The fabric was made at the mill, and Eduardo gave them a good deal; again she had no man, but the idea of one was less demanding than the reality. She considered that she and Maisie and her mother all expected to be in control yet were not keen on subservient men, demanding men being more interesting – they were all focused on careers, and it was difficult to find a suitable partner. Was she going to get in the way of the progress of the extension, or take the builder's attention away? She offered to make tea and coffee and was busy with her work. Esmeralda would interrupt the work and expect everyone's attention; Maisie, after having a quick conversation and bringing drinks and biscuits, but not without looking in the man's direction, went back into the garden. Esmeralda was occupied with her dolls and teddy bears having a make-believe picnic and talking to them. Maisie worked on her laptop. A fence had been put up before the work began the noise was continual, with music played loudly so it couldn't be heard.

Roly had given his son a job contact; in doing this the family had let him back. Verity said he had such a big family and they were talented and successful in different ways and to be that, they also had to be complicated. Beattie was almost famous in her field. Maisie had her own printing business. Maurice was a well-known boxer. Yes, Frankie had been in prison, but he was young and he would probably do well with his knowledge and skills with cars. The grandchildren were unlikely to be ordinary, and he now had another granddaughter, Esmeralda; he had accepted her and the circumstances, and the father was someone for whom he had some respect for. He called her; he didn't know if she had moved on. He hadn't progressed further at work, he could retire, and what would he do with that time? Marguerite's life and house was busy, none of the children had left. She split a long time ago with her younger partner so she was on her own.

He thought the relationship settled with living in different houses, but now he had agreed to let her move in, and she had said she would. Frankie had a test booked. Would Frankie be pleased or resent his interference? Frankie had been busy with the extension and he and Prunella had been in contact messaging and had called to the house, he had been away eighteen months and wanted to get everything right. He'd been in prison but he'd do a good job selling himself and his driving skills. He wanted to prove himself, and it was for the company to decide.

CHAPTER NINE

BEGINNINGS

Alarm bells rang when Marguerite spotted the car, a top of the range Jaguar, arriving in the drive, and watched Frankie get out; there must be a logical explanation. He walked into the kitchen.

"I have a job. I didn't tell you that I got my driving licence and Dad got me a job."

She poured two coffees and said they should go and sit down. It all sounded so good. The car went with the job, he said. She felt a little sceptical at the ease of getting a job with his record, especially a job as a driver, but she didn't want to spoil the moment. The other family members appeared and were told Frankie's news, and Colm and Maurice went out to admire the car. Frankie felt deserving of a place in the house. He'd messaged his dad, saying thanks; he knew his dad would be pleased though would not say so. He could picture him smiling to himself, thinking that ignoring him for two years would be put aside. Frankie was determined to show him, everyone, that he could be a success.

What was the business he was getting involved in? Maisie had seen the car out of the window. You didn't get a car like that to drive for no reason. There would be a price to pay, but she didn't voice any concerns; Frankie wouldn't want to hear his fears voiced, he would do his job and not ask questions, and Dad had recommended him for the job. They were surprised at that – was Dad trying to get around them by helping Frankie? They didn't approve of what Frankie had done, but they had suffered similar treatment when their father had not approved of them, so they would not have anything to do with him and should support them all; maybe Verity had encouraged him to contact him – she seemed more accepting of flaws in people. That evening they ate together. Beattie and Elodie had found a suitable meal. It reminded them of past nights when Mum's man had cooked and the air was filled with hope. Frankie thought that Prunella should know that he had a driving licence and a job. He had been drinking and after a few whiskies called to tell her his news. She was pleased, most likely anticipating some progress in their relationship, which it was not that yet and unlikely to be, but to call was acceptable for now.

Later, he sat on the side of his bed. He thought back on the day: the evening had been good, and he was getting used to being back at home. His shirt and suit, he put on a coat hanger by the open window, ready to wear the next day, and found a tie. He was concerned that he would oversleep and be late as his mind was busy, and it wasn't easy to sleep, but he was awake early. He was going for a run with Maurice; then, he would have coffee. He doubted he could eat but knew that he should, and he had to be outside the office at ten to drive Mr Spirros to Edinburgh, and hoped that everything would go well. This was his life now, and he didn't want to make any mistakes.

He was ready at 09.30, and the car started immediately; it was almost silent, just a gentle sound. He felt excited as he drove it out of the driveway. He wanted to push the car to its limits. The feeling in his stomach was almost toxic, and his breathing was hard to control. He opened the window, taking in gulps of air, and had to be careful not to speed. He slowed down when he got to the office. He was breathing normally, but felt anxious about being able to do and go anywhere. It was all so different from what he'd been used to. When he got to Edinburgh he would have time to explore while Mr Spirros dealt with business. Then, it was a long drive back. He could not have thought this day would happen in the long days while he waited for his life to begin again. Mr Spirros, a small man but heavyset, was dressed in a chequered suit that set him apart somehow. "Morning, boy." He revealed a missing tooth. He thought about his business and that he didn't have a briefcase; he got in the back, divided by a screen from the front. He watched as Mr Spirros got out his mobile phone. Frankie had the satnav set to the address – it was two and three-quarter hours. The meeting was at 1:30, allowing time to stop for coffee. Mr Spirros asked him to get two coffees, which they drank in the car.

That evening, Maisie was going to meet Brodie. He wanted to talk about what he had said about Esmeralda, but she knew he thought she was considering ending the relationship. He would say again that she and the children should move into his house, if the relationship could continue he would likely try to convince her. Brodie had done nothing to deserve this. It wasn't his fault, nothing had happened with the builder, it was just a bit of fun. At this stage she knew nothing about the man and that careless behaviour caused problems. She would listen, but knew she wouldn't move to his house. Brodie collected her from the house. His car was clean and smelt of air freshener; she liked that he was always well dressed. She couldn't fault him, the getting to know stage was always good and in the beginning she thought it would work; they had been together for some time. They had a child, but the builder had her interest now. Esmeralda was in bed. It wasn't ever a problem to go out – her mother, sister, or even Maurice was around to check on Esmeralda if she woke up, which was always a possibility.

He got out of the car and opened the door for her. He looked good and he always made an effort on her behalf, and smelt of expensive aftershave, but these good manners grated tonight – what did she want from him? He again opened the door when they got to the restaurant; she knew she was difficult to please. They were taken to a table, a waiter pulled out a chair for her. The menu and wine list brought over, Brodie ordered a bottle of expensive wine. He would have a glass, he said, the rest was for her – not a good idea; it would mean she would talk too much. But Brodie was the one to speak – he asked how their daughter was, and she said she was another Chevelly character. Brodie pointed out that she could be like him too. Maisie searched for a similarity between them. "Yes of course," she said, and poured herself a large drink which she drank. She hadn't made a decision yet. They'd been together for a long time, they had a daughter and she should move into his house, but "nothing has changed," she told him as she'd previously told Greg and she wouldn't leave the house. He had to try to convince her, said he couldn't move to a bigger house and he waited for her to think of a way they could continue. The house had a small garden, the children would have to have their own rooms. This she'd said before it was over. "Then you've decided?" She thought of how the future would be with him; he had tried as Greg had, she knew it was her – she would not leave the house, she wasn't ready; would she ever be? But her feelings for Brodie were not enough and she would of course see him when he collected and returned Esmeralda. He should be with someone more suited to him, he was a good man but now not her man. She found she felt relieved she could now pursue her interest.

Brodie looked upset but accepted that the relationship couldn't continue and he became less involved in her life. Esmeralda would not be affected and Colm wasn't concerned Brodie had not taken much of an interest in him – he had a father, a distant one, but he messaged most days; he'd been very young when he had left and he was sixteen now. He'd had a long time to adjust. Marguerite was a bit cross with Maisie, yes, she understood that you get one life, but she had spent a long time with their father, but didn't say anything as she didn't regret her younger partner or any that followed. She would meet someone right for her age and life goals. She had achieved most of hers. The business was at a manageable level; her assistant was now nearly thirty, and she saw a time when she would consider her running the shop or even Elodie – she had always liked being at the shop but was still at school and free to decide what to do in the future. She would think about it, not ready to make any decisions about the shop.

The car drove well. They arrived in good time. It wasn't his car of course, but it essentially was while he was employed. Mr Spirros was at his meeting so he waited in the car. Mr Spirros could call and he wouldn't want to wait. He called later that evening and he asked him to drive him and another man, the reason for the meeting this time unknown to him. Mr Spirros had a parcel which he locked into the glove compartment, putting the key in his pocket. Curiosity surfaced, but Frankie dismissed it; he was the chauffeur. The two men wanted to go to a restaurant. When they went in he saw through the window that there were two other men. He was told that he would have some time as the meeting could be a few hours, so he was glad that he'd eaten this morning. Nevertheless, he was hungry. Edinburgh was a town he'd not been to; going to places in Scotland was not something that any of them had done. Edinburgh was an interesting city. He'd been given a credit card – it was for petrol, lunch, anything related to his job. He found a café with outside tables. All his family and he himself liked to be outside if possible. He ordered a sandwich and a coffee, then a message on his phone said to go to the restaurant. Mr Spirros got in the car alone. Was it acceptable to ask about his boss's day? He thought that it wasn't and Mr Spirros would say if he wanted him to know. He felt he had to be careful – what was the connection between him and his father, and what did his father know? Nothing, he thought, his dad had no curiosity about other people's lives. He drove him back to the office. Mr Spirros took the parcel out of the glove box and left the key. "Well done, boy, good driving," he said. He would contact him. Frankie wanted a job for tomorrow and didn't want to have nothing to do, but he would be available if Mr Spirros called, although he couldn't drink as he didn't know when he would need to drive again. What did Mr Spirros know about him? It had been in the local papers. He messaged him that evening – it was a delivery to a man at Inverness airport the next day. What was it, he wanted to ask, thinking what it could be; he had too much time and an over imagination and sat with his thoughts.

CHAPTER TEN

COMMITMENTS

Malvina, the assistant in his mother's shop, was older than Frankie. He had not been in there for a long time for obvious reasons, and when he had, had not taken much notice of her. He'd met her once at Beattie's eighteenth and was much younger then. He decided on the way to the airport to go to the shop, being tired when he got back home in the evening, and he'd gone to his room. His mother would want to know about his day, but not about his concerns with what he was delivering. Malvina was serving a customer. She was a good looking girl. She looked at him, taking her attention away from her work. She didn't know him that well, but no doubt knew about his past. She was more his type than Prunella, and he didn't want her to think they were in a relationship. That night on his return to his home, he'd felt something – could it have been love? But he was not ready then, he wasn't ready now, he had too much to do, living for himself. He and his mother went outside to talk and when he went back in the shop he spoke to Malvina. Yes, he was pleased he was working when she said she heard he had a job. He had had virtually no contact with women while inside; there were a few female guards but they were large and unfeminine, sure that they were selected for that reason. It was a short conversation. Marguerite didn't know what she thought – he was not a suitable boyfriend for her assistant, and Prunella and her family were a part of all their lives; if it went wrong it would cause problems though she didn't think Prunella's parents knew about Frankie – maybe her mother and weren't we as mothers indulgent with daughters? He'd been in prison and not suited to the kind of life that was associated with aristocracy, but she believed in letting everything work itself out. Prunella was a nice girl; she should be with a nice boy – what had made her write to her son? He had been glad that she had made his time in prison easier but he was complicated and they couldn't be sure if he would settle to an everyday life even though he had a job doing something he enjoyed. She noticed Malvina watching Frankie as he drove away; the car alone was an attraction for girls: a rich, good looking boyfriend and a bad boy, and didn't all girls want a bad boy even if he caused trouble and broke their hearts? Did anyone actually want someone they could always feel sure of? In her family only Maurice chose quiet girls, but even then it hadn't always been right, but he was the only one married and maybe others did. Roly's girlfriend Verity but he could suddenly decide he didn't want to be with her, even though Verity suited him and was helpful to him. Malvina commented to Marguerite that Frankie was going places, which was true. She thought then that they were too closely linked. Lady Asher was a friend and a contact to Beattie, and Malvina was her assistant. Should Frankie decide to do anything. He was hardly ever in the shop, but he could decide to call in more often.

Beattie had told her about the order for the London School and that she and Maisie had hired a van which neither had driven before. They could've just got a driver to take the order to the school. After the delivery, they met Greg and Mace at a restaurant with a bar and a dance floor. They hadn't met for years, but Beattie said it was familiar, when she danced with Mace she felt differently and was now thinking it could work out, with her deciding that the rooms could be converted; but this was yet to be done going back again. They all knew how that was, but they all did it. But the work hadn't been done yet.

Occasionally Colm had been collected and then taken to England, but he was now old enough to travel alone. Maisie thought there had been enough time since they had met. They thought it would just be talking about what they had been doing, and after the evening, they would return to their lives.

Beattie recalled the visit to London. The school headmaster and his secretary were pleased with the level of personal service and the presentation of the uniforms boxed and labelled with Beattie's designs, and she was paid well. They talked about the day before, getting ready for the evening, both wanting to show that time had not changed them. At the restaurant their first impressions were that Greg was the same though he looked a bit older; Mace was as good looking, he had a small beard, his face was perhaps a little less good looking because of it – maybe he looked a little harder. He was still single but it wasn't a good idea – they had tried several times before but it always ended and the reasons why were probably the same and at the end of the evening she would liked to have taken him back, but she was sharing a room with Maisie. She could have afforded another room. When it was time to go they said they would walk them to the hotel. Maisie and Greg talked about Colm; Greg had another son now and Maisie had Esmeralda. They said goodbye inside the foyer; Beattie and Mace stayed outside. Her views on more children hadn't changed but if that's what he wanted he would have found someone to have a child with. He kissed her then pulled away.

"Beattie," he said, "I still love you."

She hesitated and then said that yes, she did too. Why was she always so careful? She had a successful business, she had a child but she didn't have a partner to share her life with. It couldn't just be left. Mace said he would call her. She got back to the room. Maisie was on her phone. She found that tears were falling. "Has it happened then, is he the one?" she said.

"Maybe he was always the one," she replied. She didn't know there had been others, she didn't understand what the problem was, overthinking the fear of being attached, so what are you now thinking; it was mixed emotions, it was never good to return to the past. On the journey back, she hardly noticed how long it took; Maisie drove most of the way. They had history but didn't know what he had been doing all these years, but he'd not found anyone else. There were a few girls, she hadn't met anyone, was with Xavier for a while, but she was too busy and it hadn't lasted. Maisie had gone in and out of relationships, thinking they were right and had two children and was now looking to start again, always in a hurry to move on to yet another relationship. There was always time, and their mother was waiting for her for ever after. It would be Mace that would move to her, he had a career but he could do that anywhere, he said her businesses were getting difficult to run and he would help her. She thought that the builder that Maisie was interested in could do some work on her room.

Maisie was in the extension, Esmeralda with her. Maisie was talking to the builder though he was still working but Esmeralda kept interrupting – she wanted her to play. Maisie gave in and left. She thought the builder would be reluctant to get involved in her inter-tangled life, her children, her family and the house; the extension was almost complete and so she would have to hurry. Esmeralda was due to start school and then he would be gone. She needed to do something. Beattie agreed to take Esmeralda with her and Elodie on a day out in the mountains, he was alone and just finishing off details; she had made coffee.

"Let's sit in the garden."

He looked for the small blonde child but she didn't appear. They sat either side of the table. She talked about the garden and how they all liked to sit in it; she continued saying that nobody understood how they didn't want to leave and they all wanted to be with someone who would want to live at the house.

His eyes looked understanding. "The house could be too small," he said, "one or both of your brothers could have children, some of the garden would probably have to be used" – they wouldn't want that but now with its new room it was big enough and they could build on top of that. The chemistry between them was there but not as yet talked of. He was here working, and she was ready to move on again. She thought of her previous relationships; she had just ended her relationship with Brodie – they couldn't continue with her still at the house. She had had a relationship with Mitac – he had chosen his family over her, he had returned to his country but he always said he would return; but she was impatient and in that time she had returned back to Greg and the choice had been made. She understood that the pull of your own country and culture was strong with Greg – they were too young to live outside the house and after many years said he couldn't stay and that her not leaving the house had been part of it, but it wasn't all of it. But the house had won. She thought he had already found someone else back in England, but she hadn't known for sure. Later she'd met Brodie and had a daughter. The builder was here to work. He suddenly took the decision from her then excuses were made for him to stay on – there was work that still needed doing. He said he would do the work for free, but Beattie said that she would pay though she would not pay until the work was done. He said he would find the time, Esmeralda was at school so they could be together. Maisie would not be working, saying she couldn't go to any meetings. Beattie's businesses were getting more difficult for her to be able to do all that was needed, but she wanted to keep control. But there were things that could be done by someone she could trust and that person would be hard to find. She would deal with it today. She hadn't contacted Mace; he was having to move and would take time to think before messaging. She wanted to sit alone in the garden and told Maisie she had her room, and she and the builder left.

Maisie was in a good mood – they could be the start of something, but Beattie knew it would end in tears; no work would be done today. Beattie sat with her laptop looking at the business and what she had to do: make sure there was enough available for the new intakes, but it ran itself, she had staff who would email her with any new orders and enquiries for uniforms, and she visited regularly twice a month and this could be just once, and who she decided on could do that. The designing was something only she could do. She had an order from Lady Asher. She hadn't seen her for a while so she would go for a visit. Maisie's attention was taken away from her work, she knew she wouldn't thank her for any criticism so she would give her a week or two. She went to the castle. Lady Asher asked her to sit on the terrace where she and Lady Asher – she always called her that; they were friends, but always respectful to her title. They talked about their daughters and she was aware of her daughter's interest in Frankie, not judgemental but her husband the Lord would expect their daughter to marry well. She wanted her daughter to be happy and Frankie came from a good background, but obviously Frankie's prison sentence and the reasons behind it couldn't be ignored. She hadn't seen Frankie for some time, and it was hard for her and most people to understand how this has happened. A broken marriage was not uncommon, but the effects on the children were different. Beattie explained about the problem with letters and numbers which had made his school work very difficult and not having a father who he could talk to. This again was something that they hadn't thought affected him, but a house full of girls and a sensitive brother had not been helpful. Frankie was a macho man. Lady Asher said her life had been restricted, but look at how she lived. Lady Asher said it would be difficult for Prunella to work out how to get Frankie. He was young and ready to kick up a different storm this time.

CHAPTER ELEVEN

RENOVATIONS

B eattie's mind was racing. The house needed some work, both her room and Maisie's. She and the builder were in love – supposedly he would move in. He wasn't concerned about his place which was a clinical apartment; both hers and Maisie's rooms could become studios with ensuites and sitting areas. Esmeralda would move into the bedroom/ playroom; it could even be divided so Elodie would have her own room and build on a study; the original had been converted into a bedroom for Colm. He wasn't a child to be concerned, he had his room and didn't need a bigger one; he was out a lot with friends from his school, maybe because he'd always spent so much time in the house. Frankie and Maurice had the use of the family bathroom and they didn't want their rooms changed. Frankie's room was a base; he was now busy and not there much. And Maurice had a girlfriend so he didn't spend much time in his room. Maurice told Marguerite that he and his girlfriend were going to get engaged – he hadn't asked her yet; it would be a long engagement. He didn't like to hurry. He was boxing and was still winning most of his fights, but there were younger boys and he had to maintain his fitness.

Mace had tried to find someone to have a family with, but couldn't commit to anyone and he would wait until the room was ready; he had things he had to do in England, and he would arrive with minimal possessions; it was set to happen. Plans had been drawn up for the renovations, and money was not an issue, though Beattie did think that now was not the time to have time away from work. She had recently found that new ideas were not easy; all her designs were original. She used some of her former ideas and modified them, so each one retained its individuality – the reason she could charge high prices; and she didn't often get asked to make dance dresses and hats that she had never really liked and didn't have the time. Malvina was interested and she had let her have her own sideline and home decor she had given to her mother and found someone to make cushions which increased the profits.

Frankie went to the office. Mr Spirros gave him a parcel. It felt heavy. He couldn't work out what was inside. Was it legitimate? Why didn't Mr Spirros tell him? He didn't want him to know, it was that simple; he was just the driver, which was also true but he was curious. He met the man outside the airport. He'd not met him before, and they went through the doors. He was intrigued and would find out at some stage – and it could just be delivering parts for a machine. Excitement was the base of his problem, he knew it would be a mistake to ask too many questions. He was enjoying the job. He liked to think he'd recovered, he didn't want to be involved in some undercover operation, which his imagination suggested he was, but a quiet life was not for him with Prunella, that would be a part of a relationship, as she had to act in a certain way; he would be expected to attend formal events, but none of this was going to happen if he could not get in the castle door. His brother Maurice would he thought to be a more suitable boyfriend for Prunella, a boxer wasn't as notorious as a car thief, and Maurice was at the point that he was considering marrying the girl that he was with – he didn't dislike her but she didn't seem significant enough to be a part of the family. Brodie as Maisie's boyfriend had been, but didn't know how he'd got her attention – again, there was nothing about him to dislike. He wanted a girlfriend but didn't want to be serious or in love; he felt he could be with Prunella and he wasn't ready for that; eighteen months in prison had taken a part of his life. He had learned a lot there about himself. He liked Malvina, but Prunella would find out Malvina was his mother's assistant. She had been watching him when he had gone to the shop. He didn't want to have to think of feelings. He'd heard that Beattie was going back – never go back they have always been told, if it didn't work the first time or the second she'd said often, she didn't know why she wouldn't commit to him, so why now? Still it was her decision, she was nearly thirty and she was old enough, and fourteen years was long enough for her to know.

CHAPTER TWELVE

WORDS

Was it devilment or was he saving himself the end result by causing total confusion, but the idea had lodged. Maurice brought his girlfriend to the house that evening. He noticed how she was dressed and looked, but that wasn't the main thing – she wasn't a suitable Chevelly wife but it was not his decision to make; protecting his brother had been prominent all his life – without him there he'd met this girl, was settling for her. She wasn't suitable for him, but he didn't exactly know why. If successful it would free him, not for Malvina but for somebody else; he invited Prunella over to the house.

She arrived looking pleased and was smiling, grabbing his hand, her large eyes hopeful. It was pointless, he didn't want to have to think of her. He then spent the whole evening encouraging conversations between her and his brother. He did have some feelings for her, but wasn't ready. He thought he was doing the right thing, but it wasn't a game he should've played. Maurice kept looking at him warningly under his breath and said, "What are you doing?"

His girlfriend was quiet and pale and Prunella was confused at the turn the evening was taking and couldn't understand why he was behaving like this – was he trying to get her out of his life? He knew he had to be alone. He would lose his motivation to succeed, wasn't ready for a relationship, and didn't want the protection of wealth. His sister's boyfriend, Mace, hadn't arrived yet; that was going to fail in his opinion. Maisie was with a man but was he right for her? He noticed him watching all the girls in the room and he said casually was she aware of her boyfriend's behaviour? The damage was done: Prunella said if he didn't want to be with her and thought he'd made a mistake he should've said. He had just got out of prison and how could he know? Yes, he had liked receiving her letters but her family wouldn't like her to be with him. She hadn't told her family and not taken him to the castle, so that was how it was left. Maurice's girlfriend had got very angry, not so quiet after all, but if she knew him she would not have behaved in that way. She was the daughter of a man who had worked himself up from a poor background and was quite wealthy herself. Maurice told him, when Frankie said she's interested in you because of money, why didn't she dress better? Then Frankie said, "Who are you to judge?" and he could've cried when his brother said he was an ex-con. Maurice went to his room and his girlfriend followed, shouting that she thought she knew him but she hadn't and she finished the relationship. He was upset but let her leave.

Maisie noticed her boyfriend looking at all the girls, and she got angry with him and how it was going wrong. He was a man, didn't they all look? He was defensive of himself. He said he wouldn't want to live in the house. She didn't trust him, and he wasn't going to do the work he had said he would, and he had then left.

What had happened was a few words out of place; how easily a relationship could be ruined; she had known him for fourteen years. Beattie questioned her decision but nothing about what he had been doing for ten years. Marguerite sat listening. She thought Frankie and Prunella were unlikely to work out because they were too different.

Maurice and his girlfriend had been happy but he wouldn't ignore Prunella – she was a friend of the family and he'd known her for years, and she, like Frankie, thought that Maurice would be a better boyfriend for Prunella; but love was indiscriminate. Mace and Beattie were going to live together, she was unsure as to how it could work – it had been years. Frankie was almost feverish, not giving himself time. He was now driving cars similar to the ones he had stolen, chauffeuring and delivering parcels, but he didn't know what was in them. The man he worked for was a contact of his father's. They had always had money. Where did that all come from? From his respectable job? She had not asked. She was sure Frankie had not meant to upset everyone. He wanted to help by bringing things to their attention. He had been away, and a lot had happened; the room was quiet now. He knew he was right – Prunella had not taken him to her parents. She couldn't accept his past. It was too much for Frankie to deal with and he'd seen his brother's girlfriend wasn't suitable. Maurice was careful with everyone's feelings and should have trusted him, he had always looked out for his brother. The relationship had ended and she left the house. Maisie would have no peace with her boyfriend. Things have a way of working out, but Frankie had now caused four relationships to end, including his own, his brother's, and Maisie's, and now the building work wouldn't be done and that would cause problems for Beattie and Mace. Chevelly House was ejecting outsiders. Maisie and Beattie were talking, Frankie had gone to his room. Marguerite left to go to hers and went out on the balcony and sat looking out into the darkness; she lit a cigarette, the smoke spiralling out. What would happen now.

CHAPTER THIRTEEN

REFLECTIONS

The domino effect had returned; it seemed.

Maisie and the builder, in the early euphoria stage, did not have enough substance to hold the relationship together and he didn't understand what she had said about the house. Maybe she had overreacted, but there wasn't anything she could do, and it was left; she took her laptop. She had work to do on the accounts and the invitations. Esmeralda was now at school, and she went into the garden. It always helped her feel better. Beattie saw her sister was on her laptop; another builder would have to do the work on the house, but she'd lost the motivation and was unsure now of her decision about Mace. Maybe she, like Maisie, had just wanted him to be right and perhaps he would be, or he would reconsider – he was leaving a life he had taken years to build; maybe the idea of it seemed possible, but the reality always something different. She would leave it and wait and that something would always decide it. She was reluctant to stop Maisie from working, which she might do if she went in the garden, but she took her laptop and sat a short distance away. Maisie acknowledged her briefly, holding up her hands.

Maurice was out running. He was angry, disliked the fact that maybe Frankie was right – had he been wrong thinking his girlfriend suitable to be his wife? He loved her or thought he did, but she'd finished it with him because he talked to Prunella; surely she could see what Frankie had been doing? She was Frankie's girlfriend. She had simply overreacted. He ran faster, pushing himself, wanting to feel the pain that would take his mind off what had happened. His mother would say leave it, let her go, to give up so easily showed that the relationship wouldn't have worked out.

Marguerite contacted Malvina to say that she wouldn't be working today. She wanted to sit on her balcony, get a coffee, her cigarettes and a book. Today she was happy to return to the escapism that she used to find books offered her. She could see her daughters both working on their laptops. Relationships had been tested again, but these were all early stages. Mace and Beattie started out a long time ago, but they needed to know more about each other's lives in the last ten years. Possibly they were meant to be together, time would tell, but their new relationship was based on the past, and a few hours in London. He was going to arrive with a suitcase, but the conversion of the room wasn't going to be done. There were other builders but no decisions would be made today.

Frankie had another delivery. This package was light. Wouldn't it be okay to ask what's in this in a joking manner? Mr Spirros seemed easy-going, but Frankie suspected he was not; he'd given him a job, not asked him any questions, left unspoken and that he wouldn't ask any either; it was a deal. He had to drive to Inverness again – was this for the same man who he was meeting at a restaurant? It was another man, who actually thanked him and said would he like a coffee. Frankie thought maybe he'd let his imagination take over, but this seemed like it was just a job though something held him back from asking the question. The package sat on the table as if it were nothing while they drank their coffees, his an americano with no milk, and the man a coffee that cost about £10. They didn't have names, another thing that didn't seem right. He could ask, it was alright for his name to be common knowledge but not theirs. He and the man talked about cars then they left. It occurred to him that the man could have collected the parcel on behalf of someone else and also didn't know what was inside, maybe his dad would know something about the company, but he would think why was Frankie looking for problems and would dismiss it.

He put it to the back of his mind. He could smell barbecue fumes as he got out of his car, the children, his sisters, his mother in the garden, Maurice cooking. They had closed ranks, no outsiders, and everyone knew how fragile Frankie was and the children were unaware of anything. They were children, so why should they be affected? They should also be told that if they asked, life could be hard. They'd had to accept things – Colm, his father leaving; he maintained contact with his dad and messaged him most days and he had his mother and a half sister, Esmeralda, who was not affected by changes, her interests more important. Elodie had her mother's support, and though she didn't meet him that often, her dad always took her out, he bought her things and wasn't concerned about where he got his money. Frankie felt relieved. He had expected them to treat him differently; they had been angry but he'd uncovered problems that were already there. He was not to blame; in his way he had been trying to do the right thing. He had a message from Prunella. She was sorry, she understood she had expected too much from him. It was too soon, and no, she hadn't brought him to the castle. Frankie replied they were both wrong, he shouldn't have done what he did. Maurice was much nicer than him, he wanted her to be happy, and perhaps he could; he had too much to do before he was ready. The messages stopped for some time.

Maurice had got a message from his ex-girlfriend. She said she had overreacted but felt they needed time apart. She said she felt out of place in his house and didn't like the feeling, she had thought she could get past it, but for now she didn't know if she could. She wanted to do other things, but neither was upset, relieved perhaps; and Maisie seemed fine and hadn't messaged him or him her. Beattie was waiting to let things unfold or fold. Marguerite enjoyed the evening – they were all together, the house was big enough for them all; they could be alone or together; nobody insisted on anything. Maybe it wasn't the usual way but what was that anyway.

CHAPTER FOURTEEN

THINKING

Beattie was working on her laptop, uploading photos of recent work she had done, and she put these on her website; it included a dress. It wasn't for anybody in particular; though in a way it was for herself and she decided to send a photo of a sketch to a fashion magazine and gave it a high price. She had not expected a reply but today she got one. It seemed a warning not to make any decisions – there was a fashion show in Milan a few months away, they would pay for her travel, a hotel and expenses, and she could take one person. She would take Maisie. The dress was just a drawing at this point, but she wasn't an unknown designer so they would have heard of her, a new face was always welcome. The dress would need to be made in size six and be worn by a model. It would be a night with famous people and music, food, and drink. She sat thinking. She had dresses for sale in Paris fashion houses, but it wasn't possible to mass produce, there were others less expensive, some more, they sold but it took time. The uniforms, her original idea, had started her business and was a regular income and an area that could grow. Maisie was not in a good mood, and now wasn't the time to tell her about Milan. It was Beattie's show, but she had two successful relationships and two children, was good with the accounts, and had success with invitation cards. Whereas she had not managed one successful relationship, she would look at all the angles.

Mace had been in the background, and in that time, she had become involved with Elodie's dad, but it had not continued. She had to go to London and thought that as she was there, she could meet Mace, and Maisie said she would like to meet Greg. They thought it wouldn't be much more than a conversation, but she got that wrong and never return to the past; she had broken that more than once. What had changed in ten years? She felt a spark; she had one child, she didn't want another but Mace was still young, and even now he could find someone to have a family with or maybe he thought he could change the direction of Beattie's life – after all, she had achieved her dream, she could be ready for something new. What was he doing overthinking, was leaving a life he has taken years to build, which he said wasn't a problem for him, but did he want to live in a room that was a studio like a hotel? It was possible to find another builder and that Maisie could let him back – she was where she wanted to be, she was not yet thirty but unsure if she would go to Milan or decide not to, but it would be a lost opportunity. Why was she hesitating? It showed she was right and not ready, but would she ever be? Maybe she was a career girl, and talking to someone would not help and it was her decision.

Maisie could find someone else in time, but now she was annoyed. She thought that maybe the builder could be the one, but looking at other women, especially in her home, perhaps she'd overreacted. She'd never really tried to explain how she felt about the house – she thought he had understood, but he didn't like being accused. People were very complicated. Understanding yourself was enough.

Beattie didn't reply to the fashion magazine immediately but continued on her laptop aimlessly, annoyed at herself. She had been offered a chance of a lifetime and why wasn't she replying? It rested on her knees. The garden was very green – it had rained more than usual. If she counted the shades of colour she would run out of fingers and toes, but in her head a dress was materialising with different layers. She sketched it then her book had slipped. She was awoken by her daughter's voice. Elodie and Colm walked from school together. She must have looked dazed.

"Are you alright, Mum? Not like you to sleep in the day." She was hungry.

"Can we make a proper dinner?" They all understood that term.

She said, "I'll get you a coffee and then we can start." She was authoritative – she had learnt that from her mother. She did most of the preparation with Beattie supervising, a message sent to the others: dinner at five.

Frankie replied that he was on his way back. Maurice in his room feeling upset at the sudden change in his relationship, thinking he had met the girl he was going to ask to marry him and was a bit thrown at what had happened. Frankie had in his way seen what his family were doing, not really aware that he had been in the wrong, but it had been too late, had caused them to look at their relationships. He wasn't angry; really, Frankie had just got out of prison, what did he know about how that had been? He hadn't thought about what he was doing or saying, but what would he do now, thinking that his life had settled? Marguerite was on the balcony. She could've called up, she was pleased to have a meal cooked, and living on snacks not the most healthy way to live.

CHAPTER FIFTEEN

ACTIVITIES

Maisie's days were her own – her children were at school, so early mornings, late afternoon and evening were busy. It was a few hours spent as before, mostly in the garden. She had appreciated the time initially, but now it left her with no meaningful way to fill it. She needed something new in her life, not necessarily someone; she thought of the builder – he had been a distraction and she had overestimated him but it no longer mattered. She never tired of the garden, it had so many areas of interest, it needed some attention, but really they all liked it wild. However, it would eventually become out of control if some basic work was not done. The grass needed cutting; she had never used the lawnmower but found it at the end of the garden. It had been left out uncovered – would it still work? She pulled at the starter; it started then gave up. Was that no petrol or was it the motor? She felt determined that she must cut the grass and then do some weeding, she needed to do something physical, not just be sat with her laptop with no plan in mind. Her eye caught the den – it had been entertainment for the boys; if they couldn't be found you would find them there, it was their escape. Colm had played there, and Elodie too. Esmeralda was less of an adventurer, she liked to play with her dolls, and now it was unused. Maisie returned to her seat at the table. She couldn't cut the grass and returned to her thoughts. Was this her life now? He had not attempted to put what had happened right and she didn't care if she was in the wrong and had offended him, and didn't they all want a compliant girlfriend? Well she wasn't that and never would be, he had insulted her with his remarks. Was she supposed to say she was sorry she didn't want to waste time – a contradiction, as that was what she was doing.

Beattie was in the kitchen when she walked in. Beattie recognised that look.

"We need a new lawnmower and garden tools."

"Do we?" and she laughed. Maisie's interest in the garden was to sit in it! She could relate, she thought her life was travelling in one direction, and now it wasn't, and she had just sent her own off in a different one. They must have the lawnmower today before she lost the motivation, she said. For an hour they sat at the kitchen table, both looking for lawnmowers, and found one that could be delivered today and a box of tools they had them somewhere, but this was easier. They both changed into work clothes, and later that day, they worked in the garden. The grass challenged the mower – it should have been cut back first. It looked a bit yellow, but it would rain and recover. Maisie left Beattie to continue, she had to go and get Esmeralda. She saw her mother immediately as she walked through the gates; she stood out with her light hair and was taller than all the other mothers. Her teacher said she could go and she ran, grabbing her mother's hand and telling her about her activities of the day.

Back at the house she felt better. She had done something useful today, and later, she was again in the garden. Esmeralda was asleep back in her room after moving downstairs into the bedroom/playroom. Esmeralda expected to be noticed all the time, she said. She had returned there, as her mum's boyfriend had gone when Mummy's room was being worked on. She would go back her thoughts, returning to him, she can't have meant anything to him, she had just been available. He may have started relationships with all the women he worked for, but she was reverting to her original concept of men – she had had two serious relationships, both resulting in a child, two affairs, none had reached an engagement or a wedding; she could have still been with Greg, but then she wouldn't have met Brodie and had Esmeralda. She regretted nothing though her handling could have been better. She had heard through Eduardo that his wife was expecting; they were married and doing everything right, but being responsible for another person... You couldn't know how you would feel until it happened; she met Eduardo occasionally. Mitac hadn't completed his college course but Eduardo had got him a job at the mill; he was responsible for international admin orders and was not involved in dealing with the materials. He had a Scottish girlfriend; she would have preferred him to be in Romania. He lived in the village, but she didn't often go there. She worked on some ideas and decided on birth announcement cards. She experimented with different weights of paper and styles of wording. She should expand party invitations – it brought in an income; she had never been paid for the accounts as she contributed to the house.

She messaged Adhara, mentioning her new idea and asking her to call around. She said it was a business opportunity, and Eduardo was now working with her father, but he would stay at the mill as long as possible and give orders even when he wasn't working there. The company had always had a blood relative running the mill. His daughter should be the next as there were no sons. She was sure Eduardo wouldn't be pleased as he was only a son-in-law, but it was the father's company, he could change the rules, but as a Spanish man, it would not be right. Somebody else dealt with the orders for twill and slight changes to keep the uniforms up to date. The looms were set by hand, a lengthy process that was interesting to watch; it had to be very precise. The twill was expensive, but the uniforms could then be worn by younger brothers and sisters as they were hard wearing. Eduardo was interested in everything regarding his career but not in his wife, at least not in his head. He couldn't resist telling Maisie of an opportunity to stray, she said he should be careful and there would be consequences. He could fall like a stone and he would, in time, get found out. Adhara said she was busy, but she would call around one evening later in the week.

Mace had been busy going through what he needed to do, but he sensed all was not well; it was not good to give Beattie time to consider. She would look at all the angles, he knew she would think her not wanting to have a child would still be a problem. They had been pleased to be together that evening, but was nostalgia working? Neither of them had met anyone and it had sounded like a good idea. He had a girlfriend in England but it wasn't serious. She was very interested in her career, though not particularly high powered so if he wanted a family he was with the wrong girls. He had his own place, which he rented, but he was going to live in a studio in Scotland, the house had been extended and had a large garden. He had travelled there throughout the years and in the first few years had waited patiently while Beattie was busy with her career and had a child. He thought that he would not get another chance, but she had not stayed with the child's father and they had again become involved; but again it had ended, when her sister's relationship with his brother had not worked out. After many years when they had both been busy with careers, now they had met again, it had been on and off so many times but this time it was different – he was going to move and live at the house, he'd planned to finish with the girl this evening. Should he upset her, the thought that Beattie could message any time, calling it off – was it true love? All of a sudden it seemed that he couldn't, yet he knew when he saw her he wouldn't be sorry, but the reality was always different and was he prepared for it to go wrong? He thought of the other family members. He had heard about Frankie; he had just been a child and he had grown up to be a troublemaker and had been in prison, and Maurice who'd always appeared soft was now a professional boxer. Maisie had ended the relationship with the father of her child, and he had heard she was with the builder in a relationship. Elodie, a teenager now, wouldn't think of him as a stepfather. She had a father, that boy, well, man, what was he doing these days? If they both wanted it to happen they'd be messaging. He didn't know what had gone on recently. He'd left a long time ago. He made up his mind he would continue in England, his family were here, though, of course they wouldn't stop him, and Greg had another child; he didn't have a child of his own. He was the favourite uncle, the only uncle, he would not want to be a part of his life. Beattie must've had the same idea. Her message arrived as his left. He read hers, and she said the builder had left, but he could return. "You know Maisie."

"Yes," he said.

"So the renovation is delayed. I've been offered a chance to show a dress, just one in the Milan show. I'm going to do that and then rethink. I know I'm overthinking. It's been ten years…" it was incomplete; his message arrived the second hers had left. They knew each other well to the point that they had messaged at the same time – could anyone know her as he did? He had said he sensed a reluctance; he knew her; it was about a child that didn't exist and may never exist and wasn't she in a house full of children? He had started to sort his life here and then thought of his parents, his brother, his nephew, and he wasn't sure; but he was sure of her though sometimes that wasn't enough. His message was incomplete and it was left.

Frankie had arranged to meet his dad to talk and to show him the car; he had only driven the Jaguar and it felt like it was his. It had made him popular with the local girls, the car that could change at any time, taken back, changed to another. It was going well. He did what he was told, nothing more. He was meeting at a coffee shop. It was one that he'd been to before. He parked

the car on the road – parking was still allowed, Scotland didn't
have yellow lines and parking permits. He noticed he'd driven out
of Scotland a few times and taken Mr Spirros to Liverpool, also
Manchester; this furthered his imagination, he had to know, then
wouldn't want to know if he found out he'd been delivering stolen
jewellery. Looking at the packaging recently, he was now thinking
it could be fake money but how could that be a registered business?
Nothing was said on their website other than offering delivery,
discretion guaranteed – that suggested something, didn't it? Could
be private papers but the size of the envelopes didn't fit with that.

His dad asked if he was wearing a new suit; yes, he wore it
for work, there was a uniform. Mr Spirros had laughed at his
expression; the last chauffeur had been twice his age and size and
said he would get one made, but said Frankie could wear what he
liked as long as he was smart. Frankie liked clothes, it seemed it
was a family trait – other than Maurice, who was always dressed
in tracksuit trousers and sweatshirts; maybe that's how he got
that girlfriend. There had been no further developments after the
evening, she had probably decided that she wouldn't want to live at
the house, it had to be the right person to fit there, all of them were
protected by it and trapped though each would say for different
reasons. Frankie liked knowing he had his family around and was
content to live in his room – after the cell it was what he got used to.

"What do Spirros Industries do?"

"You work there, Frankie, why are you asking me?"

What was his connection with them? Frankie watched his
father's face closely. He knew that he knew something, he wanted
to know. He was the one child grown up now that didn't care if
his father was upset. He watched his father's face closely, then he
caught the look. Did he care that much to be seen as respectable
and successful? That had gone when he lost his temper at the house.
What else was he capable of? "You've got a job," and he added, he
didn't know what they're doing now, but he did know what they'd

done. "They don't ask questions, do they? You're going to get asked a lot with another employer and you wouldn't be trusted with that car if he just did his job."

It wasn't a problem. He had obviously not been affected, but it was wrong that his dad judged them. He would have to be careful – he didn't want to go back inside. Perhaps he would have some respect if his dad was to tell him more, but that secrets should sometimes stay that way, like with Prunella thinking she could have a relationship with him but not telling her family. He didn't want that, and now thought that his dad had contacted the company, making it look like he was helping him, looking like he was doing something good but could turn out as anything but. He looked one more time at his dad and got ready to leave. When he'd been young maybe he hadn't cared about doing what was right, and that was why he never wanted them to get close or to get close to them and reject them one by one. Maurice had held his place, but maybe even he would fall. All they had to know was Dad considered he was right and they should be grateful for everything, where they lived, the holidays, expensive clothes, and for this reason would never look for more from him and he had not wanted to know anything that could upset him or make him think it was important to him, that his children thought him above anything bad; he knew very little about what he'd been like as a boy or a young man.

Now it seemed that his father would probably never want to speak to him again. He couldn't see he would want to either, he always claimed how important it was to be careful and to work hard, but maybe in his earlier days he hadn't been that way. "So what did you do, Dad?" He would have left but he had to know.

Roly looked away but said it was a long time ago. After that conversation was non-existent. He sensed now his connection to his dad was going to be that way – what did he have to hide? Maybe it wasn't much, but Frankie felt angry, he seemed worried but had told him nothing so there was nothing to tell the family tonight.

They were all at the house which didn't happen often, where they all went into the lounge with bowls of ice cream like they used to and they would all get a chance to say what they wanted. Beattie had news, Frankie wanted to talk about his day but it would be him upsetting the evening again. Beattie's news was about Milan and having one of her designs there.

Maisie had a lot of work recently but was she single-minded enough to reach the level of her sister's success? It wasn't a fast-growing business. Mum said Beattie would take them to heights they couldn't even think of. She was a bit annoyed at that but was accepting, knowing how she was and how much time it took Beattie's attention to her career and staying away from things that she thought would affect that goal. "We all shine in our way," she said. She made them all feel successful and at different levels, and in other careers they were.

Maurice had been visiting the castle. Prunella wanted a Chevelly boyfriend, she liked the family. Her mother agreed that Maurice would be a more suitable boyfriend than Frankie, even without his past he would not have liked the way of life. Prunella was quiet and suited to her lifestyle. Maurice was a boxer but he was well mannered. They were alike, both thought of the feelings of others. Time would tell. It wasn't that he hadn't cared, but Frankie was perceptive to his own unsuitability. He was often anxious. He had a few girlfriends but he didn't want a permanent partner. He had a talent, his job was giving him an outlet but he was not going to work for someone else, was waiting for something, he didn't know what, but he knew this job could not keep him interested indefinitely. It was the intrigue that was holding his interest now. He was always thinking of ways to find out information and was relying on a sixth sense to stop him from asking too many questions. Being in prison had taught him to be very aware of anything that might lead him into danger, the parcels had to be high value or essential papers. He didn't often take Mr Spirros these days, that he trusted Frankie and had not gone with him on any of the deliveries perhaps meant he would trust him enough to actually tell him what he did.

Beattie asked Maisie if she would like to go on the trip. Elodie and Esmeralda were cross and why couldn't they go. Elodie said she would look after Esmeralda. Money was not a problem – Beattie could afford to take them, so it was agreed it would be a girls' trip. "What about Mum?" At one time she would have leapt at the chance, but no, somebody needed to be here for Colm, he wouldn't be alone. Maurice and Frankie would be there. Marguerite knew that he wouldn't be happy to be left without his mother and his grandmother, but would be glad to have a break from his sister. She was exhausted, Marguerite knew that she could take time off but she didn't feel the need for heady excitement these days. A part of her wanted to go, but she said no, she was busy with her shop and she would meet someone one day. Her life was filled with her children and her grandchildren, and what else could she ask for?

CHAPTER SIXTEEN

THOUGHTS

There had been continual talking and rushing around that morning. The girls, excited at what was ahead, had left with their bags and got into the taxi which was waiting to take them to the airport and it was then very quiet. Marguerite was thinking, was she sorry she hadn't gone? A little nostalgic for her younger self, gradually she was becoming an age where she couldn't push herself, she was needed here. They would, in time, leave the house if it got them what they wanted. Maurice was out at the castle. Colm was in his room on the phone, talking to his school friends. Frankie was sitting with her in the garden. His anxiety was painful; she couldn't deal with it right now. She would later receive photos of the show in Milan, and they would be back soon.

CHAPTER SEVENTEEN

ALL OUT

Marguerite was on her own in the garden. It was where she did most of her thinking. She considered the very different personalities of Maisie. She had impossible expectations from any man and life in general, and Beattie separated her life into compartments; Frankie was troubled but was determined to succeed; Maurice was quieter and thought more about what he wanted to do, and he had progressed with his career. Colm was talking to his friends from school in his room.

Frankie appeared in the garden. "Mum?" he said.

"Yes?" she said, sensing she wasn't going to like this conversation. Dad she wasn't, and she waited.

He said that he didn't know him and what was he like when he was young? He saw his mother's face close, the faint lines under her eyes were as much from laughter as age and would think it was something she would have to know or tell him. He decided he would leave it to another time, she said he liked being in control or seeming to be. He had now let Verity move into his house she had heard. If Maisie settled with a partner that suited her, that would be good, not the builder. Yes, good looking, but not to be trusted. Beattie and Mace but it was too late. Never go back, though they often did. Frankie said he didn't understand them and hadn't found out anything about his father; he said he had to go to the office in the morning and had a parcel to collect.

The following day she was alone. Frankie had left Colm at school and then went with some friends to the town. It would be a while before he returned. He said "thank you for staying home" before he left, and she knew she had done the right thing.

Frankie had to collect the parcel from the office. Mr Spirros was on holiday – he didn't know where, they hadn't got past formalities. His secretary who had a room off his office had the parcel. She had never previously appeared – he hadn't known Mr Spirros had a secretary. He saw that the sealing on the package, the one on her desk, was insecure. He could have said and she would have dealt with it but he didn't and he hoped she would not notice. He could open it when he left the office. Had Mr Spirros made an error in trusting someone? The girl spoke, her voice like hot molten chocolate. Mr Spirros, she said, had given an address. He took the piece of paper from her and she picked up the parcel and gave it to him. He put it in his briefcase, which had nothing in it really, but it looked professional, and then he noticed her. Had he ever seen such a beautiful girl? He looked again. She wasn't exactly – her hair was black, very short, not many would have been able to carry that off. Her face was angular, her eyes were so light, almost transparent, her eyelashes very black. She had a long nose, a wide full-lipped mouth, her lipstick was red. What felt like an electric shock made his mouth dry. He stared at her and was winded. Her eyes narrowed. She was used to this.

"Frankie," she said.

"You," he managed to say. He picked up a glass of water that was on her desk, he held it out.

"Yes," she said.

He drank it all. She let out a little sound of laughter; it was at odds with her appearance.

She said: "Call in on your return."

Was that an invitation? She hadn't told him her name. It had to be unusual but was probably Lotty, something ordinary. Would that matter? He thought that it would. He left in the lift, his breath escaped in shudders. His hands were freezing, and beads of cold sweat had broken out, she was the sort of woman he liked, though he had not met any like her, and it was likely most men would find her noticeable, he'd like to find out about her ask her out he got in his car and sat for a while he calmed himself she looked as much trouble as he was he thought of Prunella her large eyes pale grey staring wanting him to notice her he was pleased now he had met a woman he sensed was interested in getting to know him, and thought that she would change his life.

He looked at the parcel. It was almost open, he put it in the glove box. He would find a place to look inside. The building had CCTV. He started the car. It was almost silent as he drove away. He saw a park and pulled in. He opened the window and then shut it again. He needed a cigarette. No smoking was allowed in the car, but this was a minor crime. He lit a cigarette, and the nicotine took its effect. His mind returned to the parcel – should he find out? He couldn't give the parcel like that, and he decided he would seal it and not look inside. He locked the glove compartment. It had been a day to remember, the day he'd met the woman of his dreams and there she would remain and couldn't be available, but that was for another day. Was it a test, the parcel, the girl could turn out to be Mr Spirros's wife or his daughter – he wouldn't put it past Mr Spirros to test his loyalty this way. He drove to the house and went in. He could hear the family, but he wanted to be on his own and went to his room.

The next day, he dressed carefully. He would be gone overnight, possibly two, and Maurice had a boxing match, so it would only be his mother and Colm in the house, but he was always on his phone or playing games. He would sit with her if she asked, it was just tonight and tomorrow night, and then they would be back.

She had left Malvina to run the shop, she wouldn't want to be out, she needed to be there when Colm returned home. He was sixteen, but he was still very young. She would stay at home, sit in the garden or on her balcony, and she was soon involved as photos arrived. The room had four beds and looked luxurious, the dress hung on a hanger. She messaged to cover it, thinking of Esmeralda; made from gossamer, it was dominated by red but included the colours of Scotland. That evening photos arrived which showed the venue and the dresses. The dress fell to the floor, shimmering as the light caught the diamonds which had been put on the diagonals. It had one sleeve reaching a point over the hand and trailed to the floor, the other sleeve was missing completely; the dress had been cut in such a way to show one leg. Minute shapes in leather had been sewn on indiscriminately, each a different shape and texture. It stood out amongst the other paler dresses. People would remember the dress, whether they liked it or not. A row of pink feathers around the neck, it had cost a fortune and was for sale to the highest bidder. Beattie considered the colours – for her they represented the mountain heathers. An Italian female voice translated first Italian, then French, then English, considering it was likely that all the audience would speak at least one of these. Beattie's dress was introduced with a short lead in, a Beattie design, from Scotland famous for its mountains, mills, whisky and castles, all the colours combined here. Thunderous clapping followed, hands raising as did the price – it sold for £50,000. Was this the pinnacle of her success and that she could rise no higher?

It all sounded very exciting and the photos added to the evening. As the auction reached fever pitch she was receiving messages from them all other than Esmeralda, who didn't have a phone and was complaining she didn't have one, a photo of them all together arrived, Maisie wearing the highest possible shoes that no one but she could walk in. Beattie was the only one with dark hair, the others were all blonde. She was dressed in one of her designs and Elodie wearing black trousers with a colourful jumper, and Esmeralda was in an outfit which she had put together. She had long pink socks, over black tights, a short skirt spotted in yellow and a tee shirt. All of them could've been a show on their own. She didn't know why but she sent the photo to Roly. 'The girls,' she messaged. He probably didn't know about the show, but Maurice sometimes talked to him and could have mentioned it.

Tomorrow, they would have the day to explore after they had recovered from the champagne and all the excitement. The next day, they visited Galleria Vittorio Emanuele II with its large glass ceiling arcade, a must for shopping. Then, as they didn't have much time, they took a walk in the evening in Brera, which was lit up and unique and atmospheric. Esmeralda was carried and slept and missed it all.

Frankie arrived in London. It had been a long drive on the motorway. The car drove effortlessly. He had decided to leave the parcel as it was; the man that he was delivering it to was a thin little man, with black hair that was flat and shiny with oil. He had a little moustache. He gave a smile that didn't reach his eyes, and his teeth were small. He had a few missing; he must've assumed that Frankie knew what the business was. He said to follow him and took him to a café. He chose a dark corner. It had started to rain heavily; this made it even darker. He ordered two coffees and opened the package, put his hand inside and felt the contents. They were what he was expecting to find as he didn't say anything. Frankie couldn't see what was inside; his anxiety levels were now high. He hoped it didn't show that he thought he would now find out, but it was to remain a mystery. The man put the package inside a pocket inside his coat – it must've been a very deep pocket as from the outside there was no sign of it.

The man grinned then asked, "Been to London before?"

"No," he said; he was trying to act like he was a man in control. He sipped his coffee. The cafe was hot; he could do with a shower.

77

A hotel had been booked right in the centre. He was alone but it would've been nice to share his experience. He got up to leave; the man looked up, and he got out his phone and Frankie left. He was pleased to get to the hotel. He felt anxious but he thought he had handled the meeting well. The hotel was very modern. He called room service to bring him a bottle, which arrived within minutes, and he poured himself a drink then felt himself relax. He was in London – he should go out. An hour later, wearing jeans, a shirt and a leather jacket, he sent a message saying he was going out. Marguerite messaged back, she didn't mention the girls – it was Beattie's story not hers – she would tell them when she got back.

The street was busy. It didn't matter that he was alone. You were anonymous in London – nobody cared what you were doing here and you didn't concern yourself about anyone else. He relaxed; this was a first for him, living on his nerves wasn't. Was it his time in prison had made him over anxious yet made him alert for anything, no matter how slight? What should he do? He was a long way from home. There was a bar with music. He went in, and walked straight to the bar and ordered a whisky – he could have one then one back at the hotel. He had to drive but he had a day to recover. He wouldn't want to lose his driving licence – it ensured the drink would never be a problem, for him driving was his life and would be – where it would lead from now on he had no idea. He was lost in his thoughts; he needed to eat. The bar offered snacks but he left nevertheless. It had stopped raining, and he could smell cooking. He found a steak restaurant he could sit outside. It had a covered area. He lit a cigarette and a waiter arrived with a menu then returned a few minutes later to take his order. While he waited, Frankie considered how his life had progressed. He'd discovered little about the business but his dad had made him think there was more that he should know. After the meal he ordered a coffee, then he sat for an hour then paid his bill on the credit card that he had been given. He didn't look at the cost. It wasn't his money. Later, back in his room, he switched on the TV quietly. He couldn't smoke in the room. He was suddenly exhausted. He fell into an agitated sleep where he found himself back in his cell, the photo of Prunella smiling at him. Later, a vision of a tall dark-haired girl, what was her name, but he didn't know he woke with a start temporarily disorientated.

CHAPTER EIGHTEEN

RESISTANCE

The girls arrived back in a taxi. They hadn't wanted to drive and had to park at the airport to collect the car. When they returned, a cab was always the easiest option. Their taxi friend was waiting outside; they quickly got in, they had lots of bags and had been to Milan. They were a talented, wealthy family, he recalled. When he had first met them he hadn't known why she had needed a taxi, but she had called him again often and over the years he had become someone they could rely on, he never asked for details and this assured him of more work. He drove them back to the house, they thanked him and said they would call if they needed a taxi and they went into the house.

The dress sold at a price they couldn't have imagined. It had been expensive to make, but its uniqueness made it valuable. They all talked at once and to Marguerite it was as though they'd been away and then as if they had never left, each person bringing the house back to life.

Frankie had arrived back late the previous night and was still asleep. She hadn't seen Maurice, but he had sent a message the evening before, saying he could come back if she wanted him to; she had said no, he had been at the castle and was becoming part of their lives. Roly messaged her on receiving the photo. "What a colourful crowd," he said. Did he know the extent of

Beattie's success, had she told him how much the dress had been bought for?

Later Esmeralda was in the garden playing with her dolls and had a box of clothes to dress them, reliving the show. Maisie was back in her usual seat in the garden with her laptop, looking distant, probably thinking of Milan. Elodie and Beattie had gone to their rooms; she looked in at Elodie on her way to her room, the bags next to her bed with their contents in them; she was asleep. Beattie was lying on her bed. She considered she'd been lucky, but then you made your own luck, didn't you, but time, place, and opportunity played a part.

Frankie could hear the girls in the lounge. He could call in at the office and the girl without a name could be there. He felt worried at starting what he should maybe leave, work should be separate from other things. He went into the lounge and was told about the night in Milan and how much the dress had sold for. He couldn't imagine anyone paying that much for a dress but Beattie said "actually others sold for more, nothing to a millionaire," she said.

"No," he replied, thinking was she one now, and that her keeping single worked well – maybe he should be guided by her. How was his visit to London? He told her about the hotel, the bar and his meal, but said nothing about his doubts.

Marguerite was remembering a young Roly – he'd got a part-time job. They were looking to buy a house – for this one they had savings; their parents had given them some money but they didn't quite have enough. She was pleased but hadn't asked much about what it was, he had a job that he was still doing but the salary then was not what it had finally been raised to. She hadn't questioned how he could afford on occasion when he booked another holiday, she had said casually "can you afford this?" then that look would appear. "Investments," he said, but at times it played on her mind and once she'd found a package in a drawer in their room, then only had the girls, she was curious, looking at it, trying to work out what was inside. She had then been alone later that day, the girls very young and they sometimes had a nap. She boiled a kettle, being very careful not to make the package wet. She sat at the table and opened it; inside was another package. Again she steamed it – she had to know. The package was very small; it contained a box that was sealed with Sellotape… could she possibly open it without it being noticeable? All the seals were still wet so they re-stuck easily. She replaced it. She would have to wait as the drawer was one that Roly used for spare change. She was going to the town and needed car parking money – she didn't but just before he left for work she asked him. If it was nothing he would have said to take it, he knew the package was there. He took some coins and put them on the bedside table, said he was in a rush and left. She thought of it but life was busy.

It stayed at the back of her mind until Frankie had asked what his dad was like when he was young. She had remembered how money was always available and there had been other similar packages but not in that drawer. They varied in size but she hadn't wanted to know as you couldn't unknow. Over the years she didn't think of it, nobody knocked on their door so whatever it was or had been had not brought her any cause for concern or him, but he was always closed. Had they been living under a false façade? She had an overactive imagination that trait and genetics played tricks – it had emerged in Maisie and to a greater extent in Frankie.

Maurice was at the castle; nobody did anything themselves. A maid answered the door and served dinner. They had a lot of staff, including a cook, a cleaner, a gardener, and a window cleaner – the castle had so many windows it was always time to clean them again when you got to the last one. The man had a small cottage at the end of the garden. He was the maintenance man and was always busy though he was in the background when Lord and Lady Asher entertained. It was like he had stepped into a different style of life, and it was very different to his night's boxing where all he could smell was sweat and blood. The castle smelt of lavender wax. Prunella was a nice girl, a rich girl or would be, in a way she was trapped here. The house had visitors but they were mostly her mother's age. She was a ballet dancer but not a prima donna; she trained daily. They shared that interest. She was shapely but years of dance and diet had stunted her growth. His ex-girlfriend had heard he was now Prunella's boyfriend; that made the evening seem like a lie. She had accused him that he'd been interested all along and he was not what she had thought and had been looking for a way into that life and of dubious character. Wasn't that his brother? She now had another boyfriend. They'd had a good relationship, until Frankie had caused problems. It was unfair to blame him. His mother would say it wasn't meant but were he and Prunella meant? He had feelings but truthfully he didn't feel that much for her, no excitement. He hadn't considered that important but all his family did. Maisie definitely, even Beattie with a bad boy, and he was the only one who didn't. To Frankie it was necessary in all areas of life and now he understood how Frankie had got involved. He'd always been volatile, looking for excitement, which became cars. Was there a career for him with his knowledge and that he could do better? He'd asked but Frankie said he didn't know what he was delivering and that he hadn't asked. He thought he should find out what he was involved in, always seemed edgy but he hadn't just become that way, he had always been like that. How well did he know his brother? He had seen a side of life he had no idea about.

The castle was the venue for a baby shower. Maisie's and Beattie's business contact Adhara was going to be giving birth in a week or two. Maisie had said that she didn't know why she offered, she felt a bit unfocused after the excitement of the Milan trip. A baby shower was an American concept becoming a feature in Scotland, so had the idea of baby announcement cards. It had been a success and she had American customers now. Beattie said America was further than Milan. Boxes from the shop had been provided. They were filled with gifts, baby related plus some luxury items for the mother.

Elodie was there, and Malvina from the shop, and Enid who had been the owner of the shop before she had sold it to her hadn't been at the castle since Beattie's 18th birthday. She and Malvina were both part of the family's success; there was no stopping them, each achievement better than the last and Esmeralda insisted that she should be able to go and it was easier to let her go with them.

Frankie didn't know but when he was sent to prison, it affected them all for a while. She lost interest in the shop and did nothing to increase sales. The story had been in the papers, but after a while it became old news. The shop sales increased again, and she decided to redecorate and order the latest fabrics.

Mr Spirros was back early from his holiday – had it been a holiday? – at his desk when Frankie had decided that the girl could be in the office, but the unnamed girl he was aware that she could be behind the door so he kept looking that way. Mr Spirros noticed and said she was his brother's daughter. It was a family business so even more reason to not get involved.

"So, boy, how was London?" He didn't ask Frankie about his life or how he was. "Tomorrow," he said, "I want you to fly to Prague."

Frankie felt his stomach lurch – was it excitement or fear, or perhaps both?

Mr Spirros put an envelope on the table. "Your ticket, use your card for any expenses."

The delivery was a small box and should he ask and whether Mr Spirros would expect it, but he knew and so did Mr Spirros that he wasn't in a position to; it would seem that having once been inside he would never be welcome on the outside, it followed you around like a bad smell. He picked up the box and put it in his pocket, his inside pocket. What was it, he was thinking, it could be diamonds.

"You've done well," he said and put an envelope on the table. He said to open it and inside there a were new notes; they were a bonus. He smiled at Frankie. "Have a good trip."

There was no question that he wouldn't go. He got in his car then drove away but didn't go home. He went to the park. He sat and counted the notes, how did they feel, were they real? They looked it but were they just off the printing press? He should open a bank account – if they were genuine, they would be accepted. Did they check? He thought it was unlikely. He had the rest of the day so he drove into the town – he would go to the bank where Beattie got her loan. His salary had been paid into his mother's account. He had only been paid once so now he could have his own bank account and a savings account. He was called into an office. Someone had cancelled. The man Xavier Moraity – hadn't Beattie said he'd given the loan? He had been very young then.

"Hello."

"Mr Chevelly?"

"Frankie."

"Mr Frankie Chevelly – are you related to Beattie?"

"Yes, she's my sister."

"A coincidence! How is she?"

He said, "She's famous." He said she was well known in fashion.

"So it was true, so it worked out, and is she married?" he asked.

"No, are you?"

Xavier turned his attention to business.

It wasn't the right time to ask him. He thought that if the notes weren't real, he'd be less likely to notice, so yet again he would not find out the truth though what he would do with that information if he did, he didn't know. What did he know about him, did he read the local paper? He was a businessman, and he was sure he would read about the town, but if he knew, he didn't say anything. Perhaps he was thinking of contacting Beattie again, and causing trouble for her brother would not be in his interest. He took his details. Did he have an ID? Yes he had a driving licence. Frankie took the notes out of the envelope. Xavier must have noticed they were new but didn't say anything. He could've said are they just off the printing press as a joke. His card would be sent in the post in a few days. He got up and shook Xavier's hand, showing that he was a businessman now and was trying to make a new life for himself. He saw Xavier sit back on his chair. Fate had intervened. Should he contact her again? He wasn't sure. he hadn't thought someone from the Chevelly family would be at the bank. Frankie had been a boy when he last saw him, but now he was a man.

He was going to Prague. He would need currency. He could get that here so he went up to the counter. The Czech Koruna – it was one of the few countries that still had its own currency, and Scotland still did. He had not had to fly on his own before, but he was used to being alone with a lot of people in prison yet still alone. He had been to a lot of countries, long flights but had been very young, so this was his first as an adult. All that day the small box sat in his pocket. He couldn't resist touching it, it was really eating away at his insides, thinking of what could be inside. He could so easily just open it but couldn't bring himself to. He didn't have to do this, he could just return it or he could ask but he wasn't going to. If it was later found that it was stolen or something else, he could just say he had no idea, it was his job and not for him to ask questions. The box was so small and hardly likely to be noticed. He recalled the machine you walked through, you had to take everything from your pockets. He remembered emptying his as a child, a toy, a sweet, nothing much. If you had anything metal it bleeped or would show up in your suitcase and Mr Spirros would know that he wouldn't want to get caught and would say he knew nothing and it would be for Frankie to explain. What should he do? Hope it wasn't metal? Leave it in his pocket then if asked say he had nothing in them? If it bleeped when he went through he would just say he had forgotten that he had that, could find an excuse to not go, perhaps there was other drivers but no he'd go – he was innocent after all.

CHAPTER NINETEEN

TRAVELLING

Marguerite was puzzled. Frankie was preoccupied. He was going to Prague. The job involved more than driving. He told her he was delivering a parcel, a box. What was in it, she asked, but he didn't know. She looked at him confused. It was his job, yes, but wouldn't it be better to know? Concerned about what he was involved in, she had her suspicions about an expensive car – the employer couldn't have known his past, but did he? She could tell her son was reluctant to voice his fears that it could be an undercover operation. His father had recommended Frankie for the job and said that he could be innocent, but he could also find himself back in prison.

"It's valuable," he said, "and Mr Spirros preferred to have it delivered in person."

This person being her son. They wouldn't believe that he knew nothing. She recalled his dad – maybe it had been nothing much, but it could now be something else. Even if it had been something if he was approached and the box opened and it contained a diamond. He didn't know how to handle himself, whether his fear was irrational or not. Marguerite told Beattie that he had to find out what was in the box. The door was closed. Beattie knocked, and he said to go in. Frankie was sitting on the edge of his bed with a suitcase on the floor, which contained a change of clothes. He looked up, his eyes conveying anxiety. He was her younger brother, her older younger brother. Frankie had to tell someone all his thoughts and concerns about his dad and whether this had something to do with him. Everyone thought Maurice was sensitive but he was strong. Frankie was the one of all of them who had suffered the most, he had taken a lot of bad drugs and those had left their mark, for a long time, in fact maybe the effects never left. He lived on his nerves. "We need to find out about the company." She found it and sent a message. She had a delivery to make to the London school and they asked for a uniform for a new intake. He would know her connection to her brother. It could be nothing but it obviously wasn't discretion guaranteed, but what did Mr Spirros know about the family? It could be papers it could be anything. He could have asked but he hadn't wanted to make a mistake, the box sealed in a way that it was not to be opened by anyone but the receiver. She said that it was a job and that he could get another job. The message was received almost immediately, they recommended another delivery service. "Thank you for your interest" but they didn't have a driver available. It was acceptable. Frankie was worried but it was a chance to visit Prague. Frankie liked to live dangerously but the risks were high. Was he using Frankie being an ex con to his advantage? She thought of her dad who could've once been a very different person, making money quick to further what he wanted. He had such high expectations for his own children. She would go with him. She checked the flight, booked and paid. She said she'd not been to Prague, but only just back from Milan – she liked travelling. An imagination was a gift but having an overactive imagination could be a problem, but she believed that everything worked out was true and that everything could be sorted out if and when it needed to be. Elodie had already had a few days off school so she couldn't go. It wouldn't have been right to take her – it was not known what might happen and she had just been to Milan. Maisie didn't comment that Colm had been left behind, not wanting to go to Milan.

Beattie and Frankie left the house in a taxi. The taxi driver was pleased to get the business and didn't ask about her going to the airport again so soon. The family relied on him to be available and they all called him; what they were doing or where they were going, they said if they wanted him to know. He drove to the airport and they got out and went inside. There were a number of customs officers standing around, but there was no reason why they should be noticed, though Frankie was aware he was holding his breath. But Beattie went through the machine and it didn't bleep, then Frankie followed her through and then they went into the departure lounge. Something could have happened in Prague, but again it didn't. "I need a drink of whisky," said Frankie. They found a taxi. "A good bar" – the taxi driver understood that it was early but was not too early to find one open. They clinked glasses, cheers, it was like a holiday. They had the delivery to make but there should be no problems.

Prague was a small city. They could walk; there was no need for taxis. She had put a handful of notes in his hand and he gave her a card which she put in the side of her bag. They would need him again. They had a few whiskies and Beattie called the hotel – they hadn't thought to book but they had a room. Then they had time to explore the city. It had a lot of history but they were not here for that. "Let's deliver the box then we can just be tourists." The taxi driver was there in minutes; of course he knew it was a small city. Beattie remained in the taxi when they stopped outside a jewellery shop – it was a diamond then or a precious stone. Frankie didn't care, he just wanted to deliver it. He pushed open the door. It was dark and smelt of dust. A small man with a lined face was sat at the counter on a stool; he had a monocle in his hand to study the quality of the stones. All that could've contributed to all the lines. He took the box but didn't open it. "Andreous is a good man."

Was he? Frankie shook his hand. He left the shop and got in the taxi. They were relieved that the business was dealt with and decided to go to the hotel to rest then find somewhere to eat a traditional meal. They asked the taxi driver later and he took them to a mediaeval restaurant with entertainment, belly dancers, a swordsman; the dinner was five courses. Beattie took a photo of her and Frankie, message mission completed, their glasses raised.

Back home, Marguerite was unable to concentrate. They were alright. Nothing bad had happened. Perhaps they'd never know how risky it had been, but much later in the taxi, a bit drunk and full of the good food they would not need to eat ever again, they were laughing as they said goodnight to the driver. They went to their rooms. Tomorrow they would walk around the town and buy a few souvenirs, then the taxi man would take them to the airport. "You leave so soon," he said. His eyes were very narrow, a strange colour, and his hair cut short and very blond. Beattie felt a flicker of attraction. They were leaving – she felt his eyes on her as she and Frankie walked in to the airport; she had his card, maybe, then again not she let her sensible side decide.

The family was keen to hear about their adventure and what they were involved in, but the trip to Prague had been a success, and a Czech man had her mobile number, and she was getting messages from a foreigner. Didn't she always avoid them, but he was in Prague so unlikely to disrupt Beattie's life, Maisie thought.

CHAPTER TWENTY

FAMILY REUNION

Marguerite had increased her roles; her children were adults now. They had become increasingly self-sufficient and diversified in other directions, but once you were a parent, you were always that, regardless of the age of your child. Not all, but some had found the strength to pull away from the house, and it had left them unprotected from the safety the house had given them.

They were all here today: her children, her two daughters, her two sons, and now five grandchildren and the partners of those who had them. Her eldest son didn't have children or a girlfriend he would want to include in what was considered a family day.

The house was now complete. Maisie had left a while back with the children; she didn't like his house, which was to be her new home. It was old, but she tried to make it work and stayed away from Chevelly House, but he had lied – the house wasn't his but an inheritance gift, and the owner had thought he would buy it; he had perhaps thought of this, thinking Maisie was as wealthy as her sister said they could rent or buy another house, he was a gambler in stocks and shares, and that was a problem, and he had promised a life he was unable to give, and she had returned to Chevelly House.

Beattie started a reckless phase and began a relationship with the Czech taxi driver. She was rich and no longer needed to work as much and travelled to Prague where he lived. She had been there with Frankie, and it had been fate, and she had always believed in that.

Marguerite thought that Imrich was not unlike Elodie's father in appearance, but that's where the similarities ended. She didn't need a man for money, if she ever had, she didn't know if she was a millionaire but used her money in a good way, had been so sensible for years after Zachary, her good sense overtaken then but when she became pregnant denied that her baby was his. Later he became involved in her life and accepted the child was his and now she felt this again and why couldn't she do anything she wanted? Beattie who would've told Maisie not to get involved was now with a foreigner. Elodie, a teenager, had lots of friends and was not concerned that she had less of her mother's attention these days. She always understood her mother had a business and was career-motivated, being involved in the early days going with her mother to the shop where the company had started, and meetings where she had been told she had always behaved. It was sometimes not practical for her to go, and she had school. She was always thinking of what she could do for a career, her mother had always been a fashion designer. She did what she did because it was who she was and that she should be able to do what she wanted. She had continued with her designs for the shows in Paris and Milan and then in Barcelona and Rome. Her designer dresses as her name became more well known brought in higher prices at the auctions, and her uniforms which continued bringing in business. There were uniforms for the new intakes and children grew so they needed bigger sizes. It had no limits but she had always wanted to keep control and kept it to four schools, adding a year ago another London private school which she visited regularly and would update the style to keep it fashionable. Now what she wanted to do in her spare time and how she used it was for her to decide. His eyes were narrow and the oddest colour – they weren't blue, green, grey or brown, but closest to green and pale, his features Slavic. He was just a taxi driver but no one is just anything and what they do doesn't always represent what they could do. It turned out he was a lot more, was the son of a doctor and had been expected to follow in this tradition. He had started but then taken a year out to earn some money to give him some support when he returned to his studies. He had enjoyed the freedom and he said that he was reluctant to get back to all the work and the time it would take. His father was now cross and didn't approve. He wanted him to be a doctor but it was a commitment, it wasn't a job; it was a life – he would have time for nothing else and that you sometimes weren't ready.

Chevelly House had stopped not letting in outsiders. It was always meant to be full; some had not been welcome and others had left. Beattie had the work done on her room and Maisie's, and an extension had been built on top of the playroom bedroom and that had been built a few years back. Maisie had been with the builder that she had found do the work on the house, but it had ended badly. She had done very well with her online business which was an invitation cards service that started as wedding invitations and now offered others, and had a budget selection for those that liked the idea of sending cards, but felt that was an added additional expense; this was more profitable by volume. Baby showers had some success with the gift boxes from her mother's shop, which were filled with a selection of luxury items. She had never been paid for the accounts and contributed to the costs of the refurbishments. She had when she left the house received payment. Beattie had said she needed money for her new home but she wasn't there now.

They had all settled in different ways, with different people that had taken their time, though not necessarily in a good way and Maurice had decided to retire from boxing as he wanted to be remembered as a success and there were a lot of young boxers so he continued with training other boxers. He had met his wife at one of the parties where if you could still stand after winning a fight and all you wanted to do was go home, you were expected to go. It was on one of those nights he'd met the girl who had quickly become his wife – why he had rushed he didn't know, but it seemed so hard to find the right partner. He preferred quiet girls and perhaps he wanted to marry her before the family and the house started to affect her. He now had two boys aged one and two, very close like him and his brother. As a boxer he had had an exciting career; it was challenging. You had to keep fit and after each fight you were in pain. His looks had not been ruined though he had soft features and a few scars around his eyes. The money he earned had been enough for him as he'd lived at Chevelly House but it was not enough to buy a house and look after his family. They rented a very small flat. He was used to a large house and garden; it was adequate yet inadequate.

Their wedding had been held at the castle – a connection made years back by Beattie with Lady Asher. The invitations were a gift from Maisie, the dress was made by Beattie, the dress in the lightest of tones and she was very happy with how she looked. Esmeralda behaved so well that Maisie was in tears; tiny and her determined chin set as she followed the bride, her hair pure white with sprigs of flowers and a small posy held tight in her small hands. The day had gone well and then one night in a hotel. They then returned to the flat in the evening to find it had been painted by the family with just a day to complete the task. There was no room when Samuel arrived closely followed by Oliver, and Beattie had offered to help and his mother; but he knew the upkeep of the house was expensive and all the incomes that had helped were now partially maintaining other people and other lives and he wanted to look after his own family.

Frankie's life had changed again after Prague. It had been good for Beattie but it wasn't for him – he hadn't been given an explanation other than the chauffeur had returned. He was a relative so Mr Spirros had to re-employ him. He thanked him for the time that he had worked for him and that he hoped he would find another job soon. Frankie had never been sure what the business had been and now he was not going to. He had always been concerned about what he'd been doing, but he had wanted to continue as though the whole thing had built in his head and been legal after all. He was upset; he needed a whisky. He found a cafe that was a bar and sat outside and ordered a drink then the bottle. He was still sitting there almost falling asleep when he noticed a pair of red shoes. He followed the shoes up, silk tights, long legs, a short skirt and a jumper, her hair very short and black: the girl with no name.

"Frankie," she said quietly. She sat next to him.

He could barely focus and asked what her name was. His head was starting to hurt.

"Topaz."

He remembered thinking what was she called when he'd first met her. He thought of Prunella for a moment then he slipped from his chair. He had just lost his job and his car – that was a reason for him to be drunk; this wasn't his usual behaviour. He drove for a living or had she made a call, and later he was in the back seat of a car, it was a time in his life he would always remember. He could consider that losing his job had been lucky – after all, he no longer worked for the company where she was the secretary, the niece of his previous employer – there was no need for anyone to know about them. Was there a them? Why, he asked her. "Because I don't want them to know." He knew about foreigners and some of the ways they had and he was sure he was not a good choice for her family who were Greek. Most of his family were with foreigners; Maurice was the exception with his English wife. He had been to the flat – it was very small and had no private garden, just a rough area outside. His wife with two young sons tried to keep it tidy but it smelt of damp washing which was everywhere. Maurice's wife had taken the boys to their bedroom. It was just a few feet away from where they were talking. The sofa was also a bed where they slept. His brother could have brought the family to the house.

CHAPTER
TWENTY-ONE

OBSERVATIONS

Marguerite had visited and seen the situation at her youngest son's home but hadn't said anything and she played games with the two boys. She couldn't help thinking they could have moved to the house, but Maurice said he could look after his family and move to somewhere with more room in time.

She brought clothes and toys for her grandsons, luxury items for his wife, bath products, a nice scarf, and small things that couldn't be objected to. While she was there, his wife took a bath in the small bathroom. The one at the house was large and hardly used, as Maisie's room had an ensuite as did Beattie's and she was now spending more of her time in Prague. She could work there on her designs and thought about whether she could live there, but knew that she couldn't. However, they enjoyed the time they had together; he continued with his studies and if she had appointments in Scotland would be back at the house. She travelled to fashion shows and Elodie would go with her. It was usually only a few days, so only Frankie was at the house. He had a girlfriend who was serious on his side but she was Greek and her family would not accept him. A man had been chosen for her, and couldn't change that. It wasn't a good situation. Frankie did get some work, but his interest and knowledge of cars had not yet brought him another job. He would like a garage. He now thought he should have become a mechanic, and with that skill, the eighteen months he'd spent in prison could've been overlooked; she didn't ask what he was doing and where the money came from. He was at the house most days and some evenings, as Topaz had to visit her family, and they were unaware of him. It was hardly a happy-ever-after for the relationship, which was not referred to as such.

She questioned why she didn't ask him to do some work at the house – the fence panel needed putting back, the others needed painting, and the garden required work, but he would not want her to pay him. He would say he had money, and he, like Maurice, wanted to be independent with his own money.

The house would be complete on Christmas Day, and there were now two more grandchildren, Samuel and Oliver; her grandsons were her ninth and tenth roles. When Maurice got married they could've just moved into the house and the loft, which was full of boxes converted later when the boys arrived, but he said he would be able to move in time.

For a few years, Maisie and Greg, Colm's father, lived in Maisie's room with Colm, then the study was made into a bedroom when it was time for him to have his own room. Maisie was only seventeen, and Greg was not much older – they couldn't have supported themselves, even though Greg had wanted to, and eventually, he said he couldn't stay and live his life at the house but it had not just been about the house. The relationship had ended, and later, she met Esmeralda's father, but he hadn't been able to get Maisie to move to his house with the children. It wasn't big enough, the children needed their own rooms and the relationship hadn't lasted. She was also with the builder who had worked on the house, but it hadn't worked out, so there was a time when none of them were in a relationship. Marguerite was patient and said she would meet her forever after partner, but with such a big family, even though they weren't all living in the house, there was always someone to call or message and she had her shop. Christmas Eve, she closed the shop early. Malvina, the assistant she had originally employed to work a few hours was now full-time, she had a husband and would consider her running the shop. She had no children but that could change. Malvina was sure that she wouldn't want to stay at home and would get a childminder, but there were none to consider. It was an idea for when she was ready to retire but that wouldn't be for a while yet. She went and sat in the garden with a cigarette. The garden was covered in snow; it had become very overgrown but with the snow nothing showed. In the spring she would get some work done and give Maurice a key to give to his wife so the boys could play in the garden, but when she said this to him he had said no and that she didn't drive. She then said they could get a taxi. "No," he said again. She didn't quite understand why he didn't want them to go to the house, but she had made the offer and it was left.

Maisie had met the man she had left the house for on a night out with her sister and brothers; he was a successful businessman and had a house and thought she would have to move to the house with Colm and Esmeralda. She had accepted her new life but asked why they couldn't go home, thinking it was temporary, but it could be a few years, and the children had their rooms. Maurice didn't like that the flat was small but was determined that he could change the situation himself. He didn't want any help with money. She hoped that the snow would not be a problem – the cars all had snow chains and everyone would get to the house.

CHAPTER TWENTY-TWO

RELATIONSHIPS

Christmas Day had arrived and all the family managed to get to Chevelly House. Beattie and Imrich had arrived late the night before; he was pleased he would be spending time with the family, spoke English well, and was determined he must be able to talk with the family, and they would be staying until the new year.

The relationship with the Italian had not lasted, so Maisie was back at the house; he had not told her that the house was an inheritance gift and the man who owned it wanted him to buy it; he was a gambler in stocks and shares and he always seemed to have money. It had been a short relationship and she was now starting again. Sometimes you won but he had lost, thinking that they were going to spend their lives together. He had thought she was wealthy – yes, she had money but wasn't going to spend it on a house she didn't like. Most of the children's clothes and toys had been left at the house. She never loved him, he insisted, otherwise how could she leave? She had wanted the relationship to be the one, but he'd lied and the house began to fill again.

Maurice thought he could move his family from the flat in time but agreed that in the summer, he would bring the children before he went to work so they could play in the garden as all the children had over the years. Frankie's relationship with the girl with no name continued; she was an unusual girl to look at; he said they had not met her and that in her culture a man was chosen for her and that he couldn't change it, but there was always a chance he did not allow himself to fall in love. He won in that he had the time with her, but lost as he had to let it go, he knew of pain and that it had to be experienced to understand happiness. He spent a lot of time in his room thinking, he had some money and he would accept a loan. He bought one classic car then he took it apart, each part numbered and drawn so he knew where they had to be put back. When it was ready it would be sold; it would then pay for another car. The work he did in the driveway and Imrich put back the panel that had fallen over years ago and painted the others. What next for them?

CHAPTER TWENTY-THREE

THINKING

Summer arrived and Maurice brought Samuel and Oliver to the house with their mother when the weather was good.

Marguerite now worked part-time. Malvina, her assistant, was full-time. She wasn't pregnant yet but hoped. She didn't have a long-term plan, it wasn't her way, she just wanted to enjoy more time with her grandchildren. Elodie had been at the house all her life. Colm and Esmeralda had time away but were now back.

Maurice's wife was quiet and she sat in the garden while the boys played. The garden now had a lot of flowers planted there earlier in the year and there was wildlife. The den had been cleared and it was ready to be played in, and Marguerite noticed that the swing needed a new rope. Elsbeth said she hadn't understood why Maurice hadn't wanted them to be at the house. She said he wanted to look after his family but the children should be able to play in the garden. His room was empty – it was as big as the flat they lived in and could've had work done. He wanted them to have their own home, but he didn't want any help and didn't want to own the flat.

Beattie was working on some new designs. She thought back to how it had happened. Frankie had a chauffeur job that he had got through his dad was almost sure he was involved in an undercover operation delivering stolen goods, but he wouldn't ask questions. She had made a decision and gone to Prague and she had even carried the possibly illegal delivery; she wasn't quite sure what she would've done if she had been stopped but thought she would manage to get herself out of it. A twist of fate that there were so many taxis they may never have met, but they did, she noticed him immediately but they were in Prague for a few days and she was with her brother, not the time to start something. He had her number and on her return to Scotland messages arrived daily. They got to know each other and she said she was going to go to Prague. Her family were concerned she could look after herself; she said Elodie was worried, what was she doing, was it business and if it was she could travel with her? She said another time she would take some sketches – there were several boutiques and she returned to her work. He collected her in his taxi. They had become involved; he then had to get back to his studying and she returned home.

Maisie was looking for closure, the man Ramon she had met on a night out, the builder she'd found on the internet to work on the house, she and Beattie had become mothers and had not gone out much. Beattie had considered that fate had given her the opportunity to start her career and to be with her child. Maisie's life had seemed easy with help from her boyfriend but Greg could not accept he was not responsible for them not financially, but it wasn't just that he didn't like what he considered attachment to the house and that she had refused to move and not even his son was enough to keep him there. Eventually he had returned to England. Colm had been upset but very young and he had adapted. She met Brodie and after Esmeralda was born he asked her to move to his house, but she hadn't wanted to. The relationship continued but without her moving out of the house it had failed. For a short time she had been with the builder but it hadn't lasted. She had decided

that she had to move out of the house and move in with Ramon
and that any relationship she had would fail if she stayed at the
house. One evening he opened a bottle of wine and poured her a
glass. She knew something was wrong and said when he asked she
didn't love him enough, didn't like the house and knew that he had
lied and so it was easy to leave and go back to the house.

CHAPTER
TWENTY-FOUR

REPERCUSSIONS

Y ou don't play with other people's hearts and get away with it. Maisie's ex, the Italian that she had left the house for, was a mistake, but he was not quiet and accepting.

Brodie was a Scot, and if a relationship wasn't working you accepted it; he had his daughter stay: she won, and he lost. Ramon had initially made no contact, said he was sorry, and there had been no other way. Well, there had been another way: the truth; but it didn't matter – the relationship had started with a lie. He was a gambler which was a serious problem; she wanted him to be the one and he wasn't. He had said they could rent if they couldn't buy and she had not given him a chance. He was very upset. Maisie won, and Ramon had lost. She didn't want to think back and was getting on with her life, she should have let him have his say as after that things started to happen. Maisie had re-launched her card business and baby showers; she'd thought it would take time, but after a while she was concerned as she wasn't getting any orders. She had the money from the accounts but Beattie not doing much she designed but had lost her creativity; they were both in the garden achieving nothing. Maisie didn't know what was happening with her company. Adhara, a friend, called at the house one afternoon and sat in the garden, said that she'd noticed that there were remarks on Maisie's site. One mentioned that Maisie's brother was an ex-con and there were things said about her. She didn't know if it was him but it was having an effect on the business – but why would people care if the product was good? The damage had been done though. The uniforms were still bringing in a regular income, but they needed updating. Beattie had to get her mind focused before it affected the business. It didn't take long for a winning streak to become a losing one. The house was paid for, but the cost of the renovations had been expensive, and Beattie hadn't moved her money to her savings accounts and investments. Maisie would usually tell her this must be done. She had missed the Milan fashion show. She would not show anything that wasn't as good or better than any she'd shown before. It could damage her reputation but to not have one of her designs every year, her name could be forgotten – there were always others, and Mum's waiting for a solution to show itself: Beattie's fate would decide, or Maisie ignore the situation; fate was intervening but not in a good way.

CHAPTER TWENTY-FIVE

CONVERSATION

That afternoon, a baby shower was suggested, as Adhara was expecting. She said no, she didn't know if it was a boy or a girl, and she didn't mind, but Eduardo would like a boy. Yes, Marguerite thought everyone thought that girls could be more difficult, though Frankie had tested that theory.

The shower was at the castle. It transported you to another time and place. It was free, as Adhara was a friend and a business contact through the mill where Beattie bought the twill and fabric for her uniforms or dresses. Maisie decided to add baby announcement cards to her business, which were expensive and a niche market for the rich, but she would design a more economical brand.

Enid, who owned the shop, was there and was pleased she could find out about what the family was doing. She was enjoying her retirement, and they talked about the shop. Then men were brought into the conversation – should they get on the subject? Didn't they spend too much time talking about them? If you had one you talked about him; if you didn't you talked about when you would find one. This was not true of Beattie though, who talked about business, but she said that Xavier had been in contact after not having been for a long time, as Frankie had opened his account at the bank where he worked. Xavier had asked questions. Frankie had said he was there to open a bank account and the conversation ended. Mace was probably thinking about her and the Czech and Zachary always in the background, but she wasn't in a relationship. Maisie said she had tried and didn't have the opportunity; she was at home or out at meetings and didn't often get to meet anyone. Not much was said about babies. Maisie and Beattie as mothers could remember the early weeks, but no experience was the same. The conversation was then about the house. There was no need to do the renovations but Beattie said she would in time get the work done. There was nothing much going on in any of their lives. Frankie had not been back to the office and he had not been given any more work. Mr Spirros had no idea of why they had messaged the company and he probably had not seen it as it was an automated message, a front for something else, and the last collection could still bring him trouble. He needed a job which had a future. The job had given him something to do and he had enjoyed the driving, visiting cities in Scotland and going to London and going to Prague, which had now got him to have to hide what was possibly stolen goods and he had wanted to know, but now he wouldn't find out. It had bought him into contact with the girl though nothing had come of that. He hoped that fate would offer him another opportunity. Frankie had met the girl of his dreams, he told his mother, but they were just living for now and open to whatever opportunities came their way.

CHAPTER TWENTY-SIX

RESOLVE

The time that followed was settled. Imrich helped in the garden where Beattie and Maisie had worked to bring it back to how it had looked. He had to return to his studies, and he would need no distractions if he was going to become a doctor; it was what he wanted. What place did Beattie have in this life? He said he would like a family, a son who would continue the family tradition. She didn't want to have another child, and she knew she never would. He had responsibilities, she understood and that she had won but she was to lose. After Beattie faded all the sense she had upheld and all the feelings she was heartbroken. She felt the house was in mourning – they had filled the house with the belief that true love actually existed.

CHAPTER TWENTY-SEVEN

RECOVERY

Broken hearts eventually mend; there is no timescale, and they carry a scar. They had not made a choice; the relationship could not continue. It left an untarnished memory, an occasional message to enquire about what the other was now doing would not help. She knew that returning to what was now the past was not good and she had done that herself before, but it never worked in her family. It was something they did, and it could be said it had but was it worth it? Not everyone had the chance to experience what she had, and the pain was justified. Had Maisie experienced this with any of her relationships? There was always a good reason to let them go. Beattie thought she was more upset than she was saying; she seemed to be able to shake it off and just fall in love with the next man. She said she missed him, the man she thought he'd been, but she couldn't ignore the man he actually was and she had not liked the house. Beattie thought back on past relationships – she couldn't lie here, unsure of how long she had been, he would not be doing this, he would be studying and would expect her to get on with her life. She was in the garden without her laptop, the patio doors were open, a faint smell of mixed fragrances. The perfumed air intensified as she walked further into the garden, time stood still as she thought of him, his eyes filled with pain knowing that it couldn't last; her face was wet with tears thinking of how she couldn't leave and he couldn't leave Prague. We were moveable but home wasn't – it was where you felt you belonged. Of course lots of people moved away abroad for different reasons, but she doubted if it was ever worth it. They noticed that she was in the garden and everyone now could get on without concern. Time was the only way to get back to thinking ahead and not about the past.

Maisie went out to sit in the garden after giving her some time, they were both back in the house. Maisie said she would not leave again unless it were right, but you couldn't know. It had been a risk she had not taken before and it had caused other relationships to end. They had nothing definite planned, they were recovering their strength and still young and had achieved so much, and now they didn't know what they wanted. Frankie was building his business, life had continued to challenge him; recently, the girl that he wouldn't admit that he was in love with had married the Greek man who had been chosen for her when she'd been 14 years old. Maurice, the soft one, which was how he had been thought of, was determined to live outside the house. Time would tell what was next for them.

CHAPTER TWENTY-EIGHT

CHANGES

Frankie had received a message from Mr Spirros. He asked him if he would go back to Prague. He had a delivery and he needed the money. When he told Beattie, she said she would go with him. Fate could not be ignored. They had left the house, and Marguerite was concerned that Beattie was going back – there was no point when the reasons hadn't changed. It was not good to meet or contact someone you felt strongly about but knew you could have no future with, not without considerable sacrifice. She had not ever tried to find out about the man that had ended her marriage; he wasn't to blame – she was, or more her ex-husband, but a relationship was two people so neither could be entirely at fault. She had no regrets. Maisie was looking for ideas for new businesses, and Beattie was going again to Prague. Would she contact the man? But nothing good could come of it. Adhara was at the house, Samuel was at school, and Oliver was playing. Elsbeth, Maurice's wife, had taken the opportunity to get on with some washing and tidying up the studio apartment. Maisie noticed how little Elsbeth complained, but did she have dreams? Elsbeth would say that she was at the house with the family and she couldn't expect any more. Mum assured Maisie that she would meet someone; she was always at the house though. She had met the builder, it had been a short relationship, he'd been going to do some work on the house, it had ended badly – was there a good ending? Yes, Mum would say, where you both realised despite feelings that a relationship couldn't work.

CHAPTER TWENTY-NINE

DISCUSSIONS

Some of the family were in the garden and Adhara was at the house. She didn't want to return to her own house, said it was for a family and were they not still that without him? Yes, but not a real family, she was missing her ex-husband. There had been an incident when she was expecting her second baby and it had got out of control, it had been at a party at the castle and she had finally realised what her husband was really like and she hadn't been able to stay with him. Had she made a mistake? She said no, she was assured, she said, he was always friendly and didn't know why she had got so upset, which they had seen. "He wouldn't have changed," Marguerite said and they talked about Beattie and her relationship which had been on and off over the last fourteen years though it was off again now. Xavier was waiting for Beattie. Had she been with a foreigner, had she met him when she had returned to Prague again? Maisie always in a hurry to start a new relationship but she would prefer to make mistakes and how could you know – it took years to know someone. Beattie was going to Prague. Frankie had a collection there; it was very hot today, she could see some black clouds, and it looked as though there would be a storm. She had a few hours every day to work on her businesses, she did Beattie's accounts. The income from the uniforms arrived at the start of the new school year, and sometimes there were other orders. Tomorrow she would think of a new business idea but hadn't she thought that yesterday as well.

CHAPTER THIRTY

TRAIN JOURNEY

Beattie woke with a heavy head. She felt had come to terms with their relationship, she would not leave Scotland and he had important work he had to do here; it was his destiny, he said. The window was open, she could hear the voices of people and the general sounds of activities going on. She liked Prague, but she could not live here and he had his work. Nothing about the situation could change. It wasn't her fault that the man had seen her at the cafe and told him, yet he hadn't been able to resist and called her. She hadn't changed: her family was complete and her home was in Scotland with her daughter, and he was committed to vital work in this poor country.

She called Frankie. How was he this morning, she asked. "Terrible," he groaned. Were they going to waste this time in Prague? But somehow today the city didn't capture her; she had seen what it had to offer.

Frankie had a call from his boss Mr Spirros; he'd never called before, trusting Frankie to do what was required. He had another job for a client, someone in London. He had found the jewels, he needed him to get them; that would mean getting them through customs. Frankie's head hurt and he was hungry. He could call room service but he would have to wait. What did he want him to do? Without asking, he listened: "It's a town not far from you, it's

Krakow which is in Poland, it's a long train journey or maybe you could get a taxi."

He mentioned that his sister was with him. He said he would pay any expenses but Frankie said there was no need but maybe the train tickets. The idea of travelling by train appealed, he said he'd call him back. Was he "suffering with a hung over"?

"Hang." Frankie laughed. Mr Spirros's English was sometimes not perfect; he knew him too well.

Frankie viewed himself critically in the mirror; he didn't like what he saw. He was barely thirty but he could be forty; the lines on his face pronounced, alcohol, worry, he would be old before his time. He had a shower, the hot water burnt his skin and he felt better. There was nothing that needed his attention. His specialist skills were in the restoration process; his brother was the actual businessman, and he wouldn't be missed. He was always anxious to make some contribution to his own family's lives.

There was a tap on the door. He called out yes, and Beattie opened it. She was looking very controlled. He knew that look. He said he would meet her downstairs, "call the taxi to take us to the town and find a place for breakfast en route". They stopped at the station, and he explained about the collection. She thought it would be a distraction being in this city and always had her thoughts returning to him. Frankie purchased two tickets to return; the flight was from Prague to Inverness so they would have to return to Prague. Beattie said she hadn't been to Poland before. She could add to the places she had visited. The taxi dropped them outside a café. They ordered coffee and started to feel a sense of adventure, and the following morning, they were at the railway station to get the train to Krakow.

CHAPTER THIRTY-ONE

KRAKOW

Neither of them had been to Poland before, and being on a train meant they could just sit and look out of the window; after a few hours they went to the restaurant car. On arrival in Krakow they were asked the reason for their visit – business was accepted, though looks were to the contrary. What kind of business would they be doing here? There were old taxis outside the station. It felt poorer than Prague though it had interesting architecture, a square and horse drawn carriages. They were tired and went to the hotel. In the morning they would go and pick up the collection then return to Prague. The hotel was basic, the lifts were open and rattled, slowly moving to floor two, where Frankie's room was and then to her room on the seventh floor. She felt uncomfortable; she was used to staying in luxury hotels, but it was only for one night. Talking to him had unsettled her. It was better not to return to the past. She wouldn't have, but she had to go with Frankie. The chances of her meeting him were unlikely, but fate had decided. She would meet his friend; she hadn't asked that he call. She said to Frankie they must go into the town, they had just one night and they should have a meal out. They called the Polish taxi driver. He was nice, his eyes were very blue. "Had they been to Krakow before?" He didn't speak much English but he knew the right words to use. They could go to his family's restaurant after they picked up the collection. The taxi driver drove them there and waited outside. Beattie again felt uneasy. They had to get through the border on their return to Prague, then get back to Scotland. Frankie had convinced himself that he could trust Mr Spirros, but Beattie wasn't too sure but kept the thought to herself.

It was a dusty old shop which only just about looked like a jeweller's with a few trays with rings and a glass cabinet with some necklaces and earrings. Frankie was given a very small bag. Was the shop a facade for something else? Why was she thinking this? Wasn't Frankie the one with the overactive imagination? He didn't open it; it was a bag pulled tight by string. He put it in his inside jacket pocket and no money had been exchanged.

They got back into the taxi. Their driver must have thought about what they were doing but his only concern was the taxi fare. He took them to a restaurant, and music played in the background. It was very dark with few lights and it was busy. The meal with lots of spices and rich creamy sauces was followed by dessert, a pie with ice cream. They said no to the wine, though good wines were cheap here. Frankie had a beer, Beattie a cold drink and then coffee, which was brought for them outside. A few tables with white tablecloths set with placemats and cutlery – they were taken away, the coffee put on the wood; the service was good and they smiled, hoping for a tip. Beattie added a few notes. They stayed for a while the next day, they would again travel the long journey back. No enquires were made at the station and they got on the train. The time went slowly. Eventually when they arrived they were being watched. Frankie didn't notice, thinking that the work was done. An official stopped him – what was his business in Prague? Beattie took over the conversation when Frankie looked uncomfortable. The bag was inside his pocket. They didn't look like they were tourists – they were too well dressed. She had a sketchbook in her bag. She talked to the guards and showed them her designs.

Krakow and Prague were poor cities but fashion was appreciated everywhere and there was always someone who could afford to pay. She said it was six hours on the train to visit a city and another country. She liked to travel. There was a queue and they were told to go. They walked through the barrier. Their taxi man arrived a few minutes later. He knew the times of the train and he said they had said one night – had they enjoyed their trip and it felt like it had been just business at the hotel. They sat downstairs thinking their own thoughts. She just wanted to get back to Scotland and Chevelly House. Any further contact with him would be pointless and he hadn't called again. Hearing his voice had been good but she'd been drinking and couldn't remember the conversation that well.

CHAPTER THIRTY-TWO

DISPLACED

Beattie felt uneasy as they approached the airport, and she couldn't wait to get home. They checked in online, walked through the departures, and on to the flight. Frankie talked about his cars. They landed and were soon approaching customs – anything to declare? They walked through nothing to declare and a hand was put on her shoulder. She was asked to wait. Frankie looked alarmed. Was it that had they had a good holiday? It was business. She thought Frankie shouldn't have said that, their passports showed they had been to Poland. "Can we check your bag?" She watched as he looked inside her purse, her make-up bag, inside side pockets and the outside, then looked through her suitcase. Beattie again explained about her fashions.

The official had heard of her, but he had also read a story about her family. "Your brother is a boxer."

"Was," she said.

"And another was a car thief," he joked.

She didn't say was and that they could have insisted on checking Frankie, but they didn't.

"It was nice to meet you, Miss Chevelly," he said, and they were able to leave.

Maurice was waiting for them outside. They looked pale and tired.

"Drive us home quickly," Frankie said and the car pulled away. Frankie decided his work for Mr Spirros was now over – how could they have explained? There would have been charges, they could even have taken them if he had been searched. He opened the bag and shook the jewels into his hand; they looked priceless.

Maisie was pleased they were back. She noticed their tired faces. "What happened?" she asked; they said they would sit in the garden. Mum went and sat with them. Elsbeth was getting the boys ready for bed. Elodie rushed over to her mother then there was thunder and it started to rain and there was lightning. Marguerite pulled the patio doors shut and they went in to the house

CHAPTER
THIRTY-THREE

DECISIONS

Frankie wanted to take the collection to the office. He left the following day in his classic car; he would tell Mr Spirros he couldn't do the deliveries or collections because he was too busy. It wasn't true; customs charges could've been made. Yes, he was in Prague but had that all been part of the plan that he take the risks, and he said Frankie would be able to deal with any situation. What they had collected could have been bought in Scotland or London, but would have been more expensive. Mr Spirros paid him very well and didn't he like excitement, but the thought of being locked up again… he was taking risks.

He didn't get to the office police. Cars were everywhere. The bag was in his pocket and maybe this was nothing to do with Mr Spirros but he drove away. He wasn't sure what to do so he went and parked in a carpark a short distance away and waited. Mr Spirros would contact him, he would know he was back. He needed a drink. He could hear the police sirens – had someone been arrested? Was this something to do with Mr Spirros? If it was, he would be involved. He didn't touch the bag. His fingerprints were on it already, but his anxiety was reaching fever pitch. Cold beads of sweat on his face, his clenched hands ice cold, he reached in his pocket for his cigarettes. There was nothing he could do and he decided to go to the house. The police could stop him. He pulled into the driveway and then went through the back gate to the garden; he needed to put the bag somewhere. He could get locked up for this. He hadn't asked, he was just doing what he was told, but who would believe an ex-con, a thief and he didn't even need the money. There could have been customs duties if they had been found, but that wasn't the worst that could have happened. He hoped he would call soon. He recalled the small box in the den; they always had pencils in it. It was a very wet day, nobody would go out there. He took the bag and opened the box. There was another layer, a sharpener was there. He remembered that the pencils often broke. He put the bag there and picked up a few leaves and put them on top. He then went into the house and spoke to his mother. She asked if he was alright. Yes, he was going to his room. He opened the window and he smoked. He found a bottle in a drawer and poured himself a drink and then checked his emails — had anything happened while he was away? It was just a few days. He picked up his drink. He could hear the clock that had hung on his wall since he was a boy. He found himself mentally back in his prison cell, remembering how the minutes had seemed like hours.

CHAPTER
THIRTY-FOUR

CARELESS MOVES

Frankie had been unable to settle, expecting a knock on the door, these feelings eventually subsided as it was clear that Mr Spirros had no intention of contacting him. Had he left the country? It was a mystery. He thought of the bag hidden – they may never be claimed. Curiosity was a dangerous thing that leads you where you knew you shouldn't go. He had Topaz's number, really he should have deleted it but she would most likely not mind, maybe even would like to hear his voice. He had to know – she might not know anything. His hands were shaking, he had resorted to drinking; he looked old – he had white hairs and he was barely thirty. The phone rang. Was this going to cause her a problem – but she wouldn't answer if she was with her husband.

"Frankie," that odd voice that sent shivers down his spine said, "what's wrong?"

He told her but not where he'd hidden the collection. "They're yours then." He couldn't sell them, she didn't know much; he had to be careful as he was her uncle. He was generous to the family, she said. How was he?

Frankie felt a brief measure of relief before the pain hit him. He reached for the bottle, and a glass; the whisky was like acid as it reached his stomach but he continued drinking for the rest of the day.

CHAPTER THIRTY-FIVE

REALISATIONS

The shop was closed. Malvina always opened it. She would arrive later; she didn't rush these days and had a few ideas for the shop. Malvina could be late but it was out of character. Marguerite unlocked the door. It was cold. The shop didn't match its name Haberdashery Delights – it was untidy and had a neglected air; her assistant had left in a hurry. Marguerite put away a few swatches that had been left open on the counter and straightened the shelves. Malvina was a loyal, reliable employee. She didn't want to think badly of her and there was likely a reasonable explanation and that she would call or get someone to if she couldn't call or message immediately. She noticed the money hadn't been taken to the bank which was done every day – it could have been left from the last time she was in. Was she unwell? She knew that she was back today. She made a coffee and lit a cigarette – she would hear the bell if someone called in the shop and the problem would reveal itself, but she felt uneasy. Malvina would walk in the shop. The bell rang; she got up and went back in the shop but it was a customer who asked if she had been away, how long had the shop been closed. She didn't want to say anything about why and asked what was the lady looking for. She bought some cottons and left again. Marguerite went out the back, she lit another cigarette. Something was definitely wrong but she would wait a bit longer.

Maurice partially regretted his decision to agreeing to his wife and sons going to the house, its luxury, its easiness. The flat as he now saw it through their eyes, the effects of Chevelly House starting to rest heavily on him. Keeping the house had been very important to them – his father could have forced a sale but his behaviour towards them and the fact that the house was full had stopped him and they were still at the house. None of them had much to do with him but had since been in contact when he'd recommended Frankie for a job. They were too big a family for him to cope with, his girlfriend wasn't used to a large family herself; cards and gifts arrived on the right days for birthdays but they thought it was her. They had given him the opportunities, he led a quiet life; in fact they didn't know what he did. The house was no longer an issue, his sister had paid him off, she had had work done and it was a family home. Beattie had lost what could've been her one true love because she couldn't go to Prague and become a doctor's wife; he in fact hadn't even asked her, obviously knowing that she couldn't make this sacrifice, even for him, and though she'd not said would not want to have another child – this was always a problem with her relationships and the tie to Scotland. She would not take Elodie away and Prague was not right for her child, it was backward in culture. Her mother would say the experience validated the pain, in time you only remembered what had been good.

He was still a sensitive person and if he gave in to that he would lose his motivation. He didn't like the flat but they would never get away if they returned to the house and this was how it had been with his sisters. Beattie had become successful – it hadn't stopped her but it failed her in a different way. Maisie had tried but she had given in. He didn't know exactly what Ramon had done but he knew that any man who got Maisie away from the house would probably have to lie to do it. He thought that once he got her out of the house somehow it would work out. Frankie, not wanting to be dependent on the house, was supporting himself with his classic cars, but the house was providing a place to work and stay. He'd mistaken what he felt for Prunella for love and it wasn't enough and his relationship with the girl with no name, knowing the girl was promised to another man, but he considered perhaps he could have left when he knew that it could lead nowhere, but then would always not know whether it could've worked out. It was better to try to win than lose by not trying at all. He didn't quite understand why he had to stay away, he wasn't at the flat that much; it was a base for him but for his family it was their home. Elsbeth would have moved to Chevelly House. She had spoken to Marguerite who had said that everything would sort itself in time and to be patient and wait.

CHAPTER THIRTY-SIX

TEAMWORK

Marguerite waited an hour, and then she considered the options. She had given Malvina a chance to call. She walked around the shop; it didn't look how it usually did; sometimes they were all complacent, but she was lucky and had been unlucky and that you couldn't just expect rewards to continue with no effort.

She had recently given more responsibility for the shop to her assistant; the girl seemed willing, and she paid her well. She wasn't aware of what she could earn elsewhere, but doubted money was at the root of this, not as far as the girl was concerned, and that something must have happened to make her leave the shop to go somewhere and hadn't returned. She thought it was unlikely the boys had been kidnapped; it had been years ago, and that had been related to the money. She recalled a dark tattooed man some years earlier. She had been asked to give information anonymously. She picked up the phone and called her eldest son – could he come to the shop? No, he said, he was busy, was it important? His voice distant, but he could hear the tone of her voice and said that he was on his way. He parked his classic car outside on the road as this was still allowed and went into the shop. He noticed she was on her own. They would go out the back to talk, and she shut the shop. She started talking about the past, not where he wanted to go, back to prison. He had said he'd seen a man he recognised.

"Yes," he said, "he might have been released."

She thought she had seen him in the town but hadn't been sure; however, now she was, and this could be revenge, she said. Frankie looked at his mother; she had a very active imagination, she was perceptive and how did she know him. He was going to ask her when the shop phone rang, she picked it up hoping it was Malvina or her husband and that there would be an explanation but it was a familiar voice – not one of theirs. It was him. "Your assistant £10,000." He put the phone down. She would not be able to trace the call it was too quick, but he would call again. Her face was very pale. She told Frankie what the man had said. Frankie had not been told about his and his brother's kidnapping, but he was a grown up now; it would be the time to tell him. He understood that the man was dangerous – he'd stayed in his cell trying to avoid him. This man was in their lives again. He must've known that information given anonymously had been from her; she had no choice having previously not given evidence, but when she had been asked again they said they needed her information to convict the man, she had no choice. It played on her mind but the man was locked up so she thought she could stop worrying; however, it appeared that nothing ever goes away, she said.

Frankie was agitated. The man who he had recognised had been a big part of their lives but he had been too young to remember. They were wealthy but that was a lot of money, he said. She could call the police. It was a difficult situation and she couldn't be sure the man wouldn't hurt Malvina and that everybody who appears in your life is for a reason. She said what was this man doing? He thought that she would pay, she could get the money but it would increase. She remembered the house – was Malvina there? It was a possibility. It couldn't be Frankie whom she sent – he knew him – but also it wasn't right to involve someone outside the family, this was a family problem. She had to think carefully. She had got the money before – was he sure she wouldn't involve the police? He was recently out of prison, it wouldn't take much to get put back there. The man in his younger days had cleverly avoided being caught, he was older now and maybe not as quick thinking.

She thought of Zachary, visualising him in her mind. He was Elodie's father – maybe he would know something. She contacted Beattie and said she would go to the shop; she called Zachary, and he was surprised to hear from her. She hadn't had much contact with him recently. Elodie made her own arrangements. He would send someone on a false errand. He didn't know if that man lived there, but it would be worth going to find out. Malvina's husband then called, worried his wife had disappeared; he hadn't called the police. They had had an argument, but he thought he would give her some time, and now he was concerned. He came to the shop. They were a team. He assured Marguerite that something that happened years ago wasn't her fault – how could she have known that this was going to happen again? Fear took hold at the turn in their lives; they would work it out, all of them together they could outsmart him. It was a dangerous game but it was about money, and no harm would come to Malvina as he would not jeopardise the reward. Frankie was agitated but had to remain calm; he wanted a whisky – did his mother have a bottle in the shop? She didn't know how it had got there, but she opened the cupboard in the kitchen, and there was a bottle half empty. What had her assistant been doing in the time she had left her to run the shop?! It didn't matter right now, she poured glasses of whisky; her son's eyes were feverish. Beattie said that she would like a glass, and Malvina's husband said he needed something to calm himself. They'd all driven to the shop, so only one, Marguerite said and they nodded.

CHAPTER
THIRTY-SEVEN

OUTSMART

A trick to catch a thief. Frankie recalled Mr Spirros's fake money, a bonus for work done or his silence – why should his mother pay real money? It could reveal his undercover operation never proved. Topaz was living with the Greek; a shot of pain travelled through his body – would she know someone? His present should not cross with his past. He lived on the edge of himself, he tried to focus on his car every day, he didn't say anything. They may not need to pay, they needed a villain and to act quickly Zachary sent a very respectable caller, he was an unknown, under the pretence of reading the gas meter. He had worked for them a long time ago; he had the jacket and it still fitted, even had the ID card though they wouldn't check the details and wouldn't know what the gas meter reader should be wearing. He got through the door opened by a young man – if he been told not to let anyone in he was high, he didn't care. The man had been careless and underestimated her, Malvina was in the lounge with a group of boys and a few girls. He read the meter and left. They were not sure how they could get her out. Zachary said he would go with drugs. The group wouldn't care – free drugs wouldn't be refused. They weren't, but Zachary said he'd call again the next day. He stayed for a while. The young people didn't notice when he took Malvina's hand; she was alarmed and pulled it away but he said he was here to get her out. She got up and they went into the garden; he looked back, they were all laughing and the music was playing loudly. He moved so he couldn't be seen, took Malvina in his arms and started kissing her. She had no idea what was happening or why. A boy moved and he saw them, he smiled then turned away. Zachary picked her up, threw her over the hedge and then himself; they were gone and not missed for some time.

It was evening. Marguerite had stayed in the shop with the team. He called and said that she should leave the money on the doorstep, history was to repeat but it wasn't. They all left the shop. Her big car was still useful. They went to Chevelly House. They had resolved it themselves but he knew where they lived. They sat around talking. Malvina hadn't said much about the incident and was pleased she said that nothing really bad had happened. Marguerite had avoided paying, but would he try again? There was no way of knowing what he would do and they would have to be careful. They all sat with their own thoughts.

CHAPTER THIRTY-EIGHT

PROTECTION

The house would have CCTV fitted, and the children taken to school; they were told they had to wait inside until it was time to leave. Colm said he could look after himself and said he wanted to go with his friends, but this was not allowed. Zachary would have been known as the rescuer if someone in the group remembered what had happened that night. Esmeralda was always collected from school, so other than having to wait in the headmaster's office, it was no different. He had been the headmaster when Frankie and Maurice had gone there, he had heard about the family over the years but didn't ask any questions. He said until they told him that it was no longer necessary that she could be collected from his office. They had done everything that they could. Maurice said he wouldn't be bringing the children to the house, and Frankie didn't work on his car; he had an alarm that would sound if someone touched it and even the wind could set it off. CCTV was fitted the next day.

Marguerite couldn't go to the shop and told Malvina to look for another job as she didn't know when or if the shop would open again. She decided the police should know what had happened. They recalled an incident years back. Marguerite thought the story would be too complicated for them to believe; she said that because of their wealth being at risk, the family now had CCTV she said, they had dealt with the problem themselves but if they could have a car drive past the house, the shop, and said about the house where Malvina had been taken. They said they would need to know who they were looking for, so she described him. They would provide surveillance for a week. It was very difficult to know what the man might do – he had not expected his plan to not work and many inmates on getting out would go back to what they had done before. Frankie didn't know much about the man. Zachary had said he was looking for easy ways to earn money; it was an unpredictable life and he had to be careful. He was an ex-con, not in a position to consider himself better than anyone else. The man was probably miles away and most likely he wouldn't be back, but until he was found they had done what they could. The family were told about the incident, they were well known and it had probably been easy to find out about them. You had to be careful to not upset anyone. Maisie knew it had been him who had put the remarks on her business site, but they had now stopped and she had a few orders.

Marguerite was out in the garden. She hadn't been ready to retire and did not think she would sell the shop, but would rather have someone to manage it. However, sometimes things happen to change what you thought you would do. The shop had been cleaned and put on the market. She decided to rename it Modern Draperies. The new owners could change it or even the business; there had always been a haberdashery shop in the town for as long as anyone could remember, so it was likely that it would continue as that. She would have time again for other things, then it would be like other parts of her life. She thought back, life was constantly changing, taking you off in different directions. The older children said they were being talked about. Marguerite thought that the man may not have got the money, but because of him, their lives had become more difficult. The children were told that they could walk home again and after a while, they went back to going out and Maurice decided he couldn't stay at the flat. He was no closer to moving his family to somewhere with more room and so decided to move his family to the house.

Beattie was designing again. Her work had become more well known and she was showing her new designs at shows and travelling again. Maurice had sourced cars with Frankie and Frankie did the work; the office was now being used for work and all the family were now living at Chevelly House.

CHAPTER THIRTY-NINE

READJUSTMENT

Marguerite now had so much time at home and retired before she had decided that she wanted to be. Could she have kept the shop, had she made a mistake, and should she have waited? But there had been no news that the man had been found. He could decide to return. She made the decision, got cleaners to return the shop to how it had looked, and walked around thinking of all the memories. She recalled the day she had first gone into the shop, seen an advert and called and an interview was arranged. She needed to earn some money. The owner said to call in. She had gone there. It was a haberdashery shop; it would be a few hours a day. The owner who was a family friend now had asked her if she would like to buy it as she wanted to retire. Her daughter got a loan which had now been paid.

She opened the door then locked it and got in her car. That part of her life was over now. She had changed the name to Modern Draperies and it was now sold. She had made a profit which she added to the savings she had made each month after the bills were paid. The girls covered the cost of food and the boys maintenance of the house which they did themselves if they could. Maurice, as he had his family living there, paid towards food. There were jobs that had to be done; cleaning was Maisie's job and also Elsbeth's and they had a rota. Beattie and Elodie cooked, Colm he had to cut the grass. Esmeralda was too young she said to be expected to do anything. She was told she was a day older every day and she could tidy the toys. She had given it some thought and agreed that she would.

The garden was filled with flowers. Marguerite liked to sit outside and found herself thinking she hadn't had a serious relationship for a long time other than her marriage, which now belonged to another life; then she had had a relationship with a younger man, having to divide her time between each of her roles and the shop didn't leave much time for him. It had eventually ended. She had had a few short relationships and would find her forever relationship when the time was right.

Maisie was alone. Had she missed the right one? None of them had been and she hadn't met him yet. Maisie wanted marriage but didn't want more children.

Beattie had recently gone to the bank to talk about investments and didn't expect that he would still be working there. They had met a few times over the years. She wasn't with anyone, and she could decide to meet him again. She had accepted that the time she had with the Czech could not have worked out. He was a doctor now, and she had never heard from him again. It would stop hurting, and it did in time. It was something to think of and remember.

Frankie hadn't understood why his brother had stayed at the flat as long as he had. He said he wanted to support his own family, but they had moved back to the house, and the children had the garden to play in. Elodie had started a college course and had made new friends. She'd always travelled with her mother to Milan, Paris, Barcelona and Rome. She had learnt that she was in control of her life and choices. That was an area that was fundamental, left or right, but having decided you had to believe it was where you were fated to go. Fate played tricks as did genetics, but knowing that another adventure awaited all of them, they craved that in some way.

Colm was not sure what he wanted to do. He didn't often visit his father as it was a long journey and his dad had never returned to Scotland; they kept in contact and thought it was enough.

Esmeralda, growing up now, would sometimes get angry if everything didn't go the way she thought it should, but would soon be playing with her dolls or following her mother around, demanding her attention or, if not hers, someone else's. Samuel and Oliver spent a lot of time in the garden.

A few months later they heard the man had been found and they could now get on with their lives.

CHAPTER FORTY

INVITATION

The year brought about change; the shop was sold, and because of what had happened, her assistant lost her job. She said that she would have wanted to stay on, but Marguerite preferred not to tell her about all the connections to the past; though she knew that Frankie had brought them in contact with the law and crime, the decision had been made.

Her son Maurice was back at the house with his family. She spent time with the children and his wife was pleased to not be at the flat.

Frankie had met the girl out when he thought they wouldn't meet again; when he had lost the job nobody had met her at that point – it wasn't a relationship, he said, and he explained why he was hoping the situation could change. It was a risk but Frankie liked to live like that whatever the outcome and considered that there was a chance it could work out, but it hadn't and she had married the Greek man. It was very unlikely that they would ever meet again, his time inside was becoming distant as was her time at the shop. They all had parts of life that they couldn't hold onto and Christmas was nearly here again. They usually stayed at the house, just family and partners if they had them, but this year they had received an invitation from Lord and Lady Asher, a magical day at the castle to celebrate not just Christmas but twenty years of living there. It would be a day to remember but they had no idea how memorable that day and the days that followed would be.

CHAPTER FORTY-ONE

THE FAMILY

The morning started well with breakfast in the lounge; the table set the night before and it took over the lounge. The children were sleepy and excited about the day and presents, and didn't want to have breakfast. Marguerite said that none of the presents would be opened until they had eaten a piece of toast and had a drink; the grandchildren all had blond hair, but only Oliver had dark hair. Genetics surprised you, expecting to have dark haired children; Beattie, the only one of her four children had dark hair, though Frankie's had got darker

Marguerite looked out to the garden, the snow settling and the sky heavy.

Frankie said he must go out and check the cars; the snow chains had been put on the day before Colm, her eldest grandchild, followed his uncle out of the lounge. It was crowded with all the people in the room. Marguerite pushed open the patio doors. It was snowing. The children were talking about snowmen and snowballs, the brothers varying ages and Maisie's daughter, who was still relatively young, joined in; her eldest granddaughter Elodie was on her phone, and there was a pile of gifts around the tree. Marguerite had been careful with what she had bought – the house was large but didn't have room for more possessions. Maisie said they had to get rid of some of their things but no one was listening;

that would have to be done without them knowing, they needed room to give out the gifts. Marguerite cleared the table, and then her younger son Maurice folded it away and took it out into the hall, where he leaned it against the wall. He looked at the photos of so many faces, all the members of the Chevelly family and the ones who had been part of their lives and those that now were. His dad was in the large photo of them when they were children on one of their expensive holidays. He must call his father, he knew that his father who had not liked his softness or sensitivity, appreciated it now. His father's girlfriend, who he had been with for many years, made sure birthdays and names were not forgotten, thinking it a way to keep their father in their lives.

Maisie had wrapped the gifts. Each child was given a box with their name on it, even though most were too young to read cards. In the boxes outfits in plaid and tartan for the youngest children that had been made by Beattie; later, the children lined up and they – the adult females – had tears threatening. The older boys had waistcoats and could choose the rest of their outfits, dresses had been made for Elodie and Esmeralda, and for Maisie and her mother, and she had made a dress for herself. Frankie and Maurice had dinner jackets, black trousers and satin bowties. Frankie was good looking but looked older than his years, his hair was almost grey now. Maurice had always kept fit as he had been a professional boxer.

Beattie said they should have a photo for the hall then they took their coats and scarves, hats, and gloves in the pockets and they ran to the car, trying not to get their feet covered in snow. They should've put on their boots. The snow was brushed away. Marguerite thought that comfortable shoes were important; other than Maisie who had her highest heels in her bag, the other girls were wearing flat shoes. The bags of gifts for the Lord and Lady and their family and guests were in a box in the back of one of the cars. They were ready.

CHAPTER FORTY-TWO

THOUGHTS

Mr Spirros was at his apartment which was difficult to pay for now, and he thought of how it was left with Frankie – he had been his chauffeur, and he had got him to deliver and collect parcels containing confidential items that were his cover. He'd not contacted Frankie regarding the last assignment, as he'd been investigated by the police. He had been told by Frankie's father that he had been in prison, and he asked if he could give his son a job. His father hadn't enquired what his business was now. He had done some work for him and he asked him to help his son by giving him a job, thinking that he was now a legitimate businessman and not involved in criminal activities and he'd heard Frankie hadn't had anything to do with his father for a long time, but he was not responsible for Frankie's past but it made him suitable for the work.

He was unable to continue now due to trying to deposit large amounts of cash and had been cautioned. He was not used to not having money, and as he was being watched he needed the last collection. Time had gone by and it was Christmas. Would the Chevellys be home? They could be out; he didn't want to spend the day with his family. They were all affected by circumstances as he had given them work and money. Frankie's business of renovating and selling classic cars was successful; he had helped him financially; he had given him money as it has been a way of getting rid of large amounts of cash. Frankie thought it was a bonus; he knew that Frankie probably had questions but he hadn't asked. He would drive to the house; if he was seen, he could say he was calling to say happy Christmas. He was going to relatives later in the day, but today was the only day when he thought he could call. He was not a friend and would make up a reason if asked, why he needed to talk to Frankie on his own. The house was in darkness. He got out of the car, which he parked on the road; it was snowing heavily, and his footprints were covered immediately. He looked through the lounge window. It showed that they had been there earlier but that they had gone out, there was CCTV but there was no light.

CHAPTER FORTY-THREE

THE CASTLE

The cars pulled out onto the road. It was snowing. The cars left the village, the streets were empty with a few Christmas lights around the doors. They were excited about going to the castle. Marguerite couldn't recall a Christmas Day away from the house; it was easier not to have to be at the house but she knew that something was going to happen. Had they got everything? Then the castle with pink lighting could be seen and then Lord and Lady Asher were at the door. They could feel time shifting. The smaller children had to be carried, staff took their coats and wished them a happy Christmas. It was going to be a memorable day.

CHAPTER FORTY-FOUR

AN INVITATION

Mr Spirros was still walking around the outside of the house. He saw that the door was slightly open, they must have left in a hurry and not closed it. He felt like a criminal, well he was. He pushed the door open. There was no sound; the CCTV and alarm system had not been activated – maybe the snow had caused a problem or they'd just not turned it on. He took off his boots and left them at the door. He had a torch in his pocket. It was daytime, but the light wasn't good. There was nobody around to notice but someone could be out on the road. He didn't turn on the lights. He considered what he was doing: it was Christmas Day and he was in someone's house, how low had he fallen? He was looking for something that belonged to him, but it didn't; it was stolen, valuable and the missing possession of someone else. But it was Frankie who had taken the risk and he most likely thought they belonged to him. Where would Frankie have hidden them? Did he even still have them? He thought he would, he wouldn't know what to do with them, he had stolen cars more for the adrenaline rush than the money, they would be like in his business difficult to sell.

His feet were almost silent as he went in to the house. The first door from the hall led him to the kitchen. He had no idea where to look. He knocked into a chair then he pushed a cup off the table that had been left there. He felt himself perspiring heavily. He tried to pick up the bits of broken crockery and he put them in his pocket. They could return any time but it was Christmas so they were unlikely to be back for hours or not until the evening – or perhaps they had gone away for a few days. He couldn't know, but went into the lounge where he sat on the sofa. There were unopened presents around the tree. He looked out into the garden – it was covered in snow. There was a possibility that it could have been hidden outside, but he would find nothing there today. He questioned what he was doing, he must leave. Should he shut the door? The wind could have done but it was a heavy door. No, he would leave it open. He put his boots back on, his footprints leading back to the car, which was covered in snow. He tried to pull open the car door which had frozen, but he forced it and got in. He was out of the house. He turned on the ignition but it wouldn't start.

He thought again of what he had done. He had not, he thought, left any signs of being at the house, not touched anything, but even one fingerprint could give him away. The police had those but to find them would depend on whether the Chevellys noticed anything on return to the house. He hadn't thought anyone had seen him. He tried again. This time he was able to drive away but had to stop. He waited for what seemed like ages for the car to warm up and the windows to clear, then drove away, breathing anxiously. He wanted to get back to his apartment then go to his relatives for a meal and start on the whiskies. He lit a cigarette, calming himself, then he turned on the radio. Christmas songs were playing. He had done nothing. The house was impressive, no money problems for the family, but the thought of having got away without being seen was enough. He felt quite festive all of a sudden. The car was expensive and coped well in the bad weather. He was soon back at his apartment and on the phone to his family. His nephew answered the phone: "Where are you? Dinner's at one."

CHAPTER FORTY-FIVE

AN OPEN DOOR INVITATION

The door at Chevelly House had blown open. It was a heavy door, but the wind was strong, and the snow had found its way into the house. It had melted, or most of it had, and the heating had gone off as it was on a timer. The house was cold so there were lumps of ice with the water. The hallway had carpet so it was very wet. The local police had driven by, just checking the area for anything that might be suspicious. There were crimes at Christmas with people not having money for gifts, though today it should be a quiet day and most were with family in their houses.

Early that morning they had received a call from the Chevellys' closest neighbour who had been walking her dog. She had looked around the corner of the fences. The family were very well known and she noticed the door was open. The damage to the house could've been worse if she hadn't called, but she said she hadn't closed it. The policeman who was on duty for Christmas had a phone number on file; they were known to the police. He went to the house. He saw the footprints frozen in the snow leading up to the door. He would get a footprint, he had what he needed in his car. It was very cold and it set very quickly and he managed to get the mould out without it breaking.

CHAPTER FORTY-SIX

LIGHTS ON AND OFF

The castle was decorated to a high standard. It smelt of food, candles and polish. They were being lulled in, everything had been thought of. The Christmas tree had gifts around it. There were so many, and there were gasps from the children. The lights on the tree were flickering on and off, the baubles placed perfectly, and the colours coordinated faultlessly. Marguerite looked again at the tree. Impressive as it was it could not compete with theirs at home which was decorated by the children. It told a story of the years from the childhood of her children and now her grandchildren. It was not perfectly decorated but she liked it that way. The room was warm. She was listening though not hearing what was said due to the voices around her, trying to get caught in the excitement of her family and the other guests, but she couldn't get rid of the feeling that something bad was going to happen.

The small children were sitting quietly, looking at the gifts around the tree. The Chevellys' gifts had been put to the side, still in the box. Lord Asher was talking to his wife when the room was plunged into almost darkness. Candles had been lit earlier so there was some light. He called over one of the staff and there was an announcement: there was a problem with the electrics. Everyone was quiet. He then said, "Well, this is a castle and everything is old," then smiled and there was quiet laughter and the tension eased. Suddenly the lights went back on and there were sighs of relief. They could all smell the dinner cooking some distance from the room, but without electricity, it would be ruined and it wouldn't add to the day. Christmas Day was supposed to be memorable but maybe not for those reasons. Lady Asher assured everyone that they had an old generator; it was in the basement. The lights remained on for a few minutes, and then they went off again. This time, they didn't go back on; the young children were crying. Marguerite was concerned about the problem but she knew that something else was on her mind – had they shut the door when they left? Perhaps not, but who would know.

Lord Asher hadn't returned. Frankie and Maurice, not familiar with the castle and all its rooms, suggested they go and check what was happening. But they did not know where to go. They had only been in the lounge, the dining room, the ballroom and the games room – and not there for years. They both took a candle, choosing the tallest ones. Prunella, the daughter of Lord and Lady Asher, said that she would show them where the basement was; they wouldn't find the room on their own. There were a lot, one with the generator. Prunella had, for a while, been a girlfriend to her eldest son. She'd written to him when he'd been in prison and when he'd got out. He was reluctant to get involved. He wasn't ready and not suitable for the aristocracy. Her family would not want an ex-con to be with their daughter. He'd tried to turn her attention to his brother whom he considered more suitable. He had a girlfriend he was planning on marrying but hadn't asked. That evening Frankie had, though supposedly not intentionally, caused all the relationships to end, including his own. He had ruined his brother's relationship, his sister's boyfriend he noticed was looking at all the girls and he had pointed it out to her and the evening had changed the course of their lives, but he had done it with good intentions. Maurice's girlfriend had ended the relationship, annoyed that he had been talking to Prunella and a while later he had started a relationship with her but he didn't like the lifestyle. Both her sons were friends with Prunella, who now had a more suitable boyfriend from her own background and appeared happy. Maurice was now married to Elsbeth and they had four sons.

Lady Asher gave out some gifts to the younger children to distract them, and the maid made sure all the adults had their glasses refilled. This did a lot to help, and they were all laughing at the situation. It helped ease the tension. Marguerite knew there was nothing she could do about Chevelly House and she assisted little hands in pulling at Sellotape and tried to put any thoughts to the back of her mind.

Frankie saw him first. He had slipped, the basement was damp. "Are you alright, sir?" he asked. "Anything broken?" He'd not spoken often to the Lord; he was a background figure.

Prunella was anxious about her father. The basement was very cold and dark. He said he wasn't sure. They all tried to pull him up but it wasn't going to be easy to get him back up the stairs and that he possibly needed medical attention which on Christmas Day would not be easy to get. The weather was getting worse. Lord Asher said, "We must get the generator working." His expression illuminated by a candle conveyed pain and his hands were shaking, but he didn't say anything about how much pain he was in. He was the only one who knew how to get the generator working other than their maintenance man, who was somewhere in the castle but he hadn't wanted to contact him. He had hoped his wife would find him and send him to the basement and he should've thought of that himself, but he hadn't foreseen a fall. It was Christmas and it was the man's day off.

CHAPTER FORTY-SEVEN

AN ACCIDENT

The maintenance man had been sent to the basement. He was not upset at the interruption; his rooms were without light, and he had been expecting a knock on the door. He went to the boiler room and quickly assessed the situation. Lord Asher was shaky but he didn't think he was seriously hurt, just a sprain; he hoped his smile was visible on his pale face. The generator was very noisy, but it worked; a light came on in the basement, and sounds of relief could be heard in the distance and happy voices. A disaster had been averted. Frankie and Maurice helped Lord Asher to his feet and very slowly got him back to the lounge. He waved her concerns away. "I'm fine; it was just a sprain," he said; he was settled in an armchair by the Christmas tree. The room was becoming cold as the radiators had stopped working. They would warm in a while. A blanket was found, and a glass was put in his hand. Marguerite was sitting quietly thinking what next.

CHAPTER FORTY-EIGHT

A VISITOR

The dinner was very late. The children were complaining they were hungry, and why couldn't they eat chocolate. That seemed reasonable but Marguerite knew how hyperactive children got. They had also been given glasses of Coca-Cola but they were guests, it was Christmas and not a time to say, about not eating chocolate or drinking Coca-Cola. She felt that despite the surroundings and the effort that the Lord and Lady had put in with the help of the staff, she would today have preferred to be at home. She felt out of place and her mind was busy with her thoughts regarding the house. She noticed not everyone had arrived for dinner but that time had gone and it was to be another hour. Lord Asher, who was obviously in pain, had drank a few whiskies to help. His mouth was drooped open; he was asleep – he wouldn't be pleased to be seen in this way, appearances were important to them all and they had made a lot of effort that morning. She was annoyed at her negativity. She called her daughter over. Beattie got up; she had noticed her mother had been quiet, the day had been upset by a number of things but everything that could be done had been.

She said, "What's the matter?"

"I don't know, I think I left the door open."

"Were you the last person to leave the house?" she said. "I expect someone closed it."

Marguerite looked amused at that, she said how everyone always thought someone else could or would do a particular task, when in fact nobody did.

"The house is going to be filled with snow and water," Marguerite said, then became aware that there was no internet connection. The snow and where the castle was made it unreliable; now it was off.

A place had been set at the table for someone that hadn't arrived. The doorbell could be heard. One of the maids who was standing at the drinks table left to go to the door. A few minutes later a policeman appeared. There was sounds of alarm as all the guests stared at him. Marguerite waited to hear what the policeman had to say. There had been an accident. It wasn't about the house, it was another accident. The room was quiet now. Nobody said anything, not even the children. The smaller ones were lying on the carpet, sleeping with their sticky hands clutching chocolate wrappers.

"He asked me to let you all know his phone is not working and he cannot drive. He had an accident with the car, he hit his head and I have taken him to the hospital. He says if he can he will get here later, but hopes you are having a good day and he's sorry that he has missed it."

Marguerite thought the policeman's kindness was genuine and at Christmas something that he hadn't needed to do.

CHAPTER FORTY-NINE

HIDE AND SEEK

The dinner was, despite the problem with the electrics, unaffected other than being late. The children didn't eat much – they had been eating sweets and chocolate. The adults knowing how much work it took and not having it eaten would add to how bad the day had been and they were hungry and it soaked up the alcohol. The room smelt of all the different food. The children looked hot, and not how they had when they arrived, but they sat quietly and were pleased to leave the table. The adults were taken back to the lounge which had been tidied. It was warm and the children played with their toys; the older children sat around talking. It had been a very different Christmas.

Marguerite wanted a cigarette but couldn't go outside – the snow was falling very heavily. She thought she'd never actually known there be so much before. Nobody was leaving or could arrive, but the policeman did not let the snow stop him. There was a smoking room that wasn't often used; it was at the back of the games room, but it was part of the original design of the castle, which had so many rooms that had perhaps in the past all been used. The smokers were provided with cigarette boxes; there were cigars, coffee was served, boiling water for tea with different tea bags and plates of biscuits, and one of the staff stayed in the room. After they had left the room was cleared.

The children were taken through to the games room by the maid. Their toys had been tidied away and old fashioned party games were organised for the younger children – pass the parcel, expensive gifts inside as they took off the wrapping. It was fun. They were laughing and trying to snatch the parcel when it wasn't their turn. It was Christmas and the children didn't understand any of what had gone on. Musical chairs followed by a game of hide and seek – was that a good idea? They had been told to keep to the lower floor but the number of hiding places they had to choose from gave them lots of places to hide and it was hard to find them. The younger ones in the most obvious places and then leapt out to shout here I am! Elodie and Esmeralda were looking for them, they were laughing and having a good time; they found all the boys apart from Samuel – where was he? They searched everywhere. Half an hour went by, then an hour, and Elodie was thinking he could have hurt himself. Esmeralda said that he was clever and kept looking in even more unusual places. The adults joined in looking for him. They knew he was somewhere, had he fallen or was he sleeping in a corner in a cupboard? Lady Asher kept apologising. It had not been a good idea. "The castle is so big."

It was now almost time for tea being prepared. Unaware of the situation they were looking in every possible place where he could have hidden, then the gong sounded to tell the guests that tea was going to be served. But nobody felt like eating now, very concerned. "He must've heard it."

They were relieved when he appeared – "where were you hiding?" he was asked, pushing away hugs. It was a game and you weren't meant to be found, but he couldn't wait any longer, he said, and also he couldn't tell them in case he might hide there again. They all laughed, couldn't believe his patience. He was given a gift; inside was a truck. The other boys looked on. Lady Asher pulled out a bag from behind a chair. It was a lucky dip, she had thought of everything.

The Christmas tea included many different sandwiches piled high on silver plates, and there were cakes, some that possibly they had never even seen or tasted before, and there were jellies in different colours. On the backs of each chair ribbons had been tied in Christmas colours, silver, gold, red and green; and even their names on cards put on the chairs. Whatever had happened or hadn't it was a memorable day.

CHAPTER FIFTY

FURTHER DEVELOPMENTS

At the castle they were surprised to get a visit from the police again.

"Mrs Chevelly, you left your door open."

"You were right," Beattie said to her mother.

"It's now shut." He spoke very slowly so as not to shock. "There are footprints leading to the door and as it's been so cold they were frozen, so I've got a mould. I don't know how much good it would do, but it's evidence," he said. "We would need to get fingerprints, and I need your permission to do this. Tomorrow I can go to the house with some others to check the house."

The thought that it had been burgled was on their minds, and whether there was any damage.

The policeman continued, "You cannot return to the home until this is done; I know you will want to get back, but you must wait."

Marguerite nodded and gave him the key. Lady Asher said that they could, of course, stay. Other than the Chevellys, the other guests had left, and how eventful this Christmas was turning out to be and not in a good way. The Lord and Lady had done everything they could. Marguerite thanked them. Procedures must be followed.

CHAPTER FIFTY-ONE

WAITING

It was not going to be possible to leave that evening. There was more food served in another of the rooms of the castle where they could play cards and listen to music. Could they eat any more? They felt they must try. The older children said they wanted to stay up, though they liked the idea of sleeping in one of the many bedrooms which had been prepared in case they stayed. Lady Asher had thought of everything; the boys were all tired and taken to a bedroom by the maid so in the morning they could play with all the toys. Lord Asher looked very pale. He had a bedroom on the first floor that had been prepared as he would not be able to get to the main bedroom which was on the fourth, and he was not seen again by any of the guests the following day. He was in more pain. The day went by slowly but they had to wait, and the staff continued with food and drinks. The children played another night at the castle and then they would be able to go back to the house.

CHAPTER FIFTY-TWO

CHEVELLY HOUSE

He looked serious but that didn't mean anything. The police were trained to not give anything away. Marguerite got out of one of the cars with Frankie; the others stayed in the cars. Nobody was allowed to go in. They could see the footprints in the snow but it was turning to slush now. The policeman handed back the house key and they walked in. The carpet was wet and would need to be replaced. They went into the kitchen. Marguerite noticed a cup had been broken and cleared away there were a few small bits of broken crockery on the floor. They said they had fingerprints from the chair, nothing else had been touched. They then went through into the lounge, which had gifts that hadn't been opened. There was an indent in the sofa but they could've done that so who had been in the house? Someone in the area that knew them? The weather had been cold and there were cars in the drive other than the ones they had driven to the castle. They didn't know who it could have been – someone looking for something but then hadn't known where to look? The policeman waited but neither of them said anything. "If you think of anything or anyone who may have been in the house please call us, but as nothing has actually been damaged or taken we're not too sure if there was actually a case," he said.

"Let's get everyone in. We can talk later." Marguerite knew that this involved Frankie, and he thought he knew who it had been. It could have been someone who didn't know them, and it would reveal itself in time. She watched Frankie as he walked over to the drinks cabinet, took out a glass, and poured himself a drink. Marguerite went outside. The others were already out waiting the hall carpet. "It's wet," she said. Any of the children that could be carried were, the others walked in. Elodie asked if it was bad, they wanted to know if anything had been stolen. They waited for an answer. Marguerite smiled and reassured them and they all laughed when she just said "no, it's a mystery".

CHAPTER FIFTY-THREE

QUESTIONS

Frankie was standing outside the patio doors, smoking a cigarette. In his other hand was a drink. He was looking out into the garden. The snow was untouched. This, it seemed, was what he had wanted to find. He said, "Whoever had been at the house hadn't gone in the garden."

"Why would anyone go in the garden?" Something was hidden out there – perhaps she would not ask. "No," she said. It was cold. They should go in; he said that he would but stayed in the garden and lit another cigarette. He had tried to get past all that had happened. He now had his own business, the house was cold. Had anyone put on the heating? Yes. Had it been her that had left it open? With so many other people there who could have? There was more to know.

CHAPTER FIFTY-FOUR

DAMAGES

The carpet was ruined but Maisie said that they could claim on the insurance. Beattie said the stair carpet would be a different colour to the hall, so that would have to be replaced. It was for accidental damage, but the door was left open, so it might not be considered as that. They were a wealthy family and could afford to pay. They asked Marguerite what she thought of two colours, brown and red. "No," she said.

They went back to looking but nothing suitable was found, so it was left. Maurice and Colm pulled out the carpet from the hall. It would have to be taken away, and the carpet on the stairs was left until they had made a decision. Nothing had been taken, though it wasn't good that someone had been in their house, and it had been a very cold day. You would not have thought that anybody would have been out and someone who knew them would have closed the door. They went into the lounge and opened all the presents. Maisie told the children to choose some toys they didn't play with to give away, and they considered what could be.

CHAPTER FIFTY-FIVE

INVESTIGATIONS

Mr Spirros had a good Christmas and was thinking he would restart a business. It would have to be legitimate but he would need money again. He thought of the last collection and its valuable contents – should he make contact with Frankie? But then he would know it had been him at the house. Though he thought it unlikely that he could decide to face the consequences and tell the police about him, that he was being watched, he perhaps might be pleased to give them back. He would think about what he should do, which he hadn't done by going to the house.

The snow in the garden was almost gone; Frankie it would seem was waiting for that, and Marguerite decided that something was hidden in the garden and it was someone Frankie knew who'd been in the house. Most of their cars were in the drive, and they could have been in and said he was calling to wish them a happy Christmas, but to find an open door was an invitation to go in the house. He wasn't a thief as he hadn't taken the electrical goods.

The police called and said they had traced the fingerprints to a man who had been in trouble with the police years back. They had not charged him but he had more recently been cautioned about money laundering; he was someone they had been watching and said they always keep the information. Marguerite remembered thinking she would have preferred it if they hadn't and there was more to know and it involved Frankie; they were making enquiries regarding what had happened and would call if they had any further information. She had a conversation with Frankie and told him what had been said. He thought he had got past all that had happened being in prison and he had his business and it could remain unsolved.

She said to Beattie that she should talk to him and they went into the town and found a cafe with tables outside. It was cold but people sat outside so they could smoke, and there was usually someone but today nobody had. They wouldn't want anyone to hear them. Frankie told Beattie that nobody else knew about the last collection and he had not been contacted and it had seemed as though it would not be found. He didn't think the children went in the den – there were other things to do in the garden. He was surprised that it hadn't been found but thought if one of the children had they would have told someone. Was it still there? He didn't know. He had put it to the back of his mind. We should find out and then decide what to do. Beattie, noticing again how much older than his age Frankie looked, said that he had a good life. He nodded, thinking of how he could now mess it up and the consequences if this man was arrested and had to tell the truth he would be involved, and she'd been with him on the delivery and collection. She would think very carefully before any decisions were made.

The police called Mr Spirros. He thought that nothing further would happen and didn't ask why they asked him to go the station. When he got there he was asked to give a footprint. He knew that he'd been caught out thinking the snow would have covered them, but it had been very cold and frozen the footprints. He couldn't refuse and he didn't show any nerves externally why had he gone to the house. He knew the family, Frankie, he said. They knew of Frankie's involvement with crime but he was reformed and a successful businessman and they didn't need to know that Frankie had worked for him. "I just thought as it was Christmas it would be nice to visit," he said.

Should he have just walked into somebody's house?

"The door was open, and you left it open for someone else to go in."

Mr Spirros didn't reply straight away, then he said that "no he shouldn't have".

They would check his story and he was allowed to leave. Nothing had been taken and the door had been open and there was no crime and there was nothing more that could be done. Mr Spirros got into his car but he needed to be very careful.

Marguerite was told by the police that the man had been calling to say happy Christmas to the family but could not give a name as there was no crime. That was enough for Frankie to know who it had been, but he had made no further contact, so it had stayed where he had hidden it. There were no decisions to be made.

Another year was beginning, and they would all return to their work, and what had happened would not be forgotten, but thought of as not that important; the carpets could be replaced, and nothing had been taken. Frankie remained distracted for a while, but whatever he thought would happen didn't, and he seemed less agitated. The year had been very eventful, and there had been a lot of changes. You couldn't know what would make you take another path and if it was the right one, but sometimes it seemed that you had no choice. It had been a while since they had all left the house for any reason other than at Christmas and could not have known how it would turn out. Marguerite went out onto the balcony wearing a coat and her cigarettes in her pocket. She thought they should think about a holiday. It would need to be a large property. She would discuss it with the family. It was very cold, and it would be good to look forward to going away. The year had not been good for the Lord, and Lady Asher called and asked what had happened at the house. She said that nothing had been taken by the man, and no, they didn't know who it was, someone who knew them had called to say happy Christmas, how was the Lord? "It was a Christmas they hadn't expected," she said. He was back at the castle and he would recover; in time they would be inviting people for the new year and they would get an invitation to go.

They had all taken risks, maybe chosen the wrong paths. Frankie knew who had been at the house. The police could have told him, but it would be kept on file and he couldn't give a name. Frankie had recognised the man in prison who had been in their lives as an uninvited guest at a party, but surnames were not used. They were there to think about the errors in their ways, there were endless hours to do that but he had used the time in a good way; he went to the gym. It tired him. The lights went off at 10pm, the nights were long alone with your thoughts, but many returned to their old lives. He didn't want to have his freedom taken away. The police said there had been no crime so that the box would stay hidden. Maurice returned with his family to the house, and Maisie was at the house after another relationship that hadn't worked; Beattie was designing. The new year was beginning. Win, Lose, Rise, Fall, mystery and intrigue and foreign places, memories good and bad, her thoughts returning to the events of the year.

They were called on to their flight as a group and were all sat together, they and all the other passengers were strapped in. There was quiet talking. It was a tense moment, you felt the plane's wheels align and heard nothing but the roar of the engine, you were thrown back in your seat as the plane left the runway. They were off on an adventure so what was next for them?

www.ingramcontent.com/pod-product-compliance
Lightning Source LLC
Chambersburg PA
CBHW070549180626
46817CB00005B/1765